"Where did you learn to do that?"

"What? Tidy my hair?"

"No. Halter a bull. Not many women can do that. Lots of men can't, in fact."

Virnie chuckled. "Surprised you, didn't I?"

Conor laughed, too. "You could say that."

"I have to admit, it feels good to surprise Conor Russell."

"Why is that?" He moved closer. In the light from the open door she saw his eyes were dark and watchful.

She met his look without revealing any sign of how her nerves jittered at having him so close.

"Because you have it all figured out. Women are weak and useless. There is no place for them on the farm or in your life. And pretty things have no value."

He didn't speak or indicate how her statement affected him.

"Maybe I proved you wrong."

Books by Linda Ford

Love Inspired Historical

The Road to Love
The Journey Home
The Path to Her Heart
Dakota Child
The Cowboy's Baby
Dakota Cowboy
Christmas Under Western Skies
  "A Cowboy's Christmas"
Dakota Father
Prairie Cowboy

LINDA FORD

shares her life with her rancher husband, a grown son, a live-in client she provides care for and a yappy parrot. She and her husband raised a family of fourteen children, ten adopted, providing her with plenty of opportunity to experience God's love and faithfulness. They had their share of adventures, as well. Taking twelve kids in a motor home on a three-thousand-mile road trip would be high on the list. They live in Alberta, Canada, close enough to the Rockies to admire them every day. She enjoys writing stories that reveal God's wondrous love through the lives of her characters.

Linda enjoys hearing from readers. Contact her at linda@lindaford.org or check out her website at www.lindaford.org, where you can also catch her blog, which often carries glimpses of both her writing activities and family life.

LINDA FORD

PRAIRIE *Cowboy*

Steeple
Hill®

Published by Steeple Hill Books™

STEEPLE HILL BOOKS

Steeple
Hill®

Recycling programs
for this product may
not exist in your area.

ISBN-13: 978-0-373-82860-9

PRAIRIE COWBOY

www.SteepleHill.com

Printed in U.S.A.

I have loved thee with an everlasting love:
therefore, with lovingkindness have I drawn thee.
—*Jeremiah* 31:3

Dedicated to the teachers who have touched my life and the lives of my children in a positive way and especially to godly teachers who both teach and live a Christian example. May you be blessed in your work.

Chapter One

Dakota Territory, 1886

Her dream was about to come true in living, vibrant color.

In a few minutes she would welcome her first class of students. Eighteen-year-old Virnie White stood in the doorway of the brave little white schoolhouse and watched the children arriving in the schoolyard. The brittle yellow grass had been shaved by one of the fathers and the children's feet kicked up soft puffs of dusty mown grass.

A horse entered the gate of the sagging page wire fence. The rider, a man, reached behind him. A child grabbed his arm and dropped to the ground.

The boy wore overalls that looked as if the only iron to touch them had been a hot wind. He wore a floppy hat that did little to hide the mop of wild brown curls. He needed to be introduced to a pair of scissors.

Virnie expected the father to ride away as soon as the boy got to his feet but he hesitated, glancing about until he saw her in the doorway. She felt his demanding look and gathered her skirts in one hand and hurried across the yard. He dismounted at her approach. She held out her hand to the black-haired man. "Miss Virnie White, the new teacher."

He took her hand in his large, work-worn grasp and squeezed. "Conor Russell."

She pulled her hand to her side. "And this is…?" The boy raced over to join the boys in kicking around a lump of sod.

"Ray."

"How old is Ray?"

"Eight."

At the note of longing in the man's voice, Virnie turned. His gaze followed his son, concern evident in the tense lines around his eyes and the way he pressed his lips together. She studied him more closely. A handsome man with thick black hair that needed trimming almost as much as his son's, eyebrows as black as his hair, and dark blue eyes that shifted toward her, giving her a look as full of challenge as the superintendent had given at her interview.

She lifted her chin, clasped her hands together and met the man's look without flinching.

"Ray…well, Ray is…" He shifted his gaze past her to the men in the wheat field bordering the schoolyard.

She'd watched them earlier as they tossed stooks into the wagon and had breathed in the delightful nutty scent of ripe grain.

"What I'm trying to say is Ray's mother is dead."

One thought vibrated through her brain. A widowed father who cared about his child. She wanted to squeeze his hand and tell him how noble and wonderful he was. But the knowledge of his concern picked at a brittle scar and somewhere behind her heart a tear formed. Willing herself to ignore the place that held those hurtful things, she tipped her chin higher. Her lips felt stiff as she spoke. "Mr. Russell, rest assured I shall treat Ray with kindness and fairness." As she intended to treat all the children.

He touched the brim of his hat in a gentlemanly expression that made her feel she had given him the assurance he needed. "I hope so." He swung back into the saddle and kicked his horse forward, urging the animal to a gallop as soon as he left the schoolyard.

She stared across the field to where the men worked. The creak of the wagon as it groaned under the weight of stooks made little impression on her conscious thoughts.

Four little boys, Ray among them, raced past her chasing the steadily shrinking clump of sod. Did the child realize how fortunate he was? But then he was a boy. Obviously not the same thing to deal with as a motherless girl.

Virnie pulled herself back from the ghost of her past and with clipped steps headed for the schoolhouse. She glanced at the empty bell turret. How pleasant it would be to ring a large bell by means of a rope, but the community could not yet afford one so instead she picked up a hand bell from the step where she'd left it.

At its ringing, the children hurried toward her.

"Girls on my right. Boys on my left."

They quickly sorted themselves out except for Karl and Max who didn't appear to understand English.

She went to the pair and pointed them toward the boys' line. She counted the boys—only eight and she knew at last count there were nine boys and eight girls. She checked the girls' line and immediately saw the problem.

"Ray, the boys are in this line."

Several of the children tittered and Ray shot her a blazing look.

Hilda, twelve and the oldest Morgan girl, leaned over and whispered. "Ray is a girl. Rachael Russell. It's just her pa doesn't know what to do with a little girl."

Shock burned through her veins as hot and furious as the prairie fires she'd read about with a shiver of fear. Her vision alternated between red and black. She feared she would collapse. No. She couldn't do that. Not on her first day of being a better-than-average teacher. She sucked in a breath, amazed the rush of air did nothing to dispel her dizziness. She knew firsthand how it felt to have your father wish you were a boy. Her father had gone so far as to say it. "Too bad you weren't a boy. Would have made life simpler."

How could she have run so forcibly into such a blatant, painful reminder of her past? A past she had vowed to completely forget? And she would forget it.

Miss Price had rescued her, taught her to be a lady, and modeled how to be a good teacher. She was here to emulate Miss Price.

Lord God, give strength to my limbs and forgetfulness to my thoughts.

She straightened her spine and went to the little girl. "Rachael, what a beautiful name. I'm sorry for my mistake."

The child ducked her head, hiding her face beneath the brim of her hat.

Virnie gently removed the hat. Her eyes widened as a wave of brown curls fell midway down the child's back. "Why, what beautiful hair you have."

Rachael sent her a shy look of appreciation.

Something in the child's eyes went straight to Virnie's heart and pulled the scab completely from her wound. Her past stared at her through the eyes of Rachael Russell. And in that heartbeat of time, Virnie knew she had come to Sterling, North Dakota, for a reason as noble and necessary as teaching pioneer children. She had set her thoughts to becoming a dedicated teacher who found ways to challenge each student to do his or her best. Those who needed the most help would be her special concern. Those who excelled would receive all the encouragement she could provide. She'd make Miss Price proud of her by imitating her noble character as a teacher.

But just as Miss Price had done seven years ago when she saw Virnie's need and reached out to help her, she'd repeat the way Miss Price had helped her by reaching out to Rachael and perhaps repay her by doing so.

Her mind made up, she welcomed the children and had them march inside where she proceeded to get them into grades according to some rudimentary testing. Karl and Max Schmidt were problems. She couldn't test them when the only things they said were, "My name is Karl," or, "My name is Max," and, "Please." But here was her first challenge. Teach these two to communicate in English.

Correction. Her second challenge. Rachael was her first.

During the lunch break, she whispered to Hilda

that Rachael's hair would look beautiful brushed. She gave Hilda ribbons. Hilda smiled and nodded. A bright girl. And before the lunch break ended, she'd fixed Rachael's hair and so no one would realize it was for her benefit, she redid her two little sisters' hair as well.

When the school day ended and Virnie dismissed the children, Rachael hung back waiting for the others to leave before she sidled up to Virnie.

"Teacher, thank you for the ribbons."

Virnie touched Rachael's head. "I don't need them any longer. You enjoy them."

"I will." She raced outdoors.

Virnie followed.

Conor had no call to get Rae. She was perfectly capable of finding her way home. Had for two years now. But he wanted to see the new schoolmarm again. All day her face had filled his thoughts. Was she really as pretty as his memories said? He muttered mocking words. He knew pretty was use- less out here. How did it help anyone create a solid home?

It seemed all the other children had left but he waited on horseback for Rae to exit. She ran out, the new school teacher at her heels.

Yup. Just as pretty as he recalled. Her hair was a doe-soft brown and pulled back into a bun. He couldn't say for sure if her eyes were brown, only that they were dark and watchful and this morning he'd decided she had a kind look. Soft, too. He could tell just looking at her. He'd give her a month, two at the most, before she found life a little too much work on the wild prairie and turned tail and ran. Took a special woman to survive frontier life and Miss White didn't have the hardy look at all.

Without even glancing at Rae, he reached down and pulled her up behind him then touched the brim of his hat by way of greeting to the schoolmarm. As he tugged the reins and left the schoolyard he wondered why she gave him such a disapproving look.

"How was your day?" he asked his daughter.

"Good."

"You like the new teacher?"

"Yeah, Pa."

He didn't say more as he thought of that pretty new teacher. Now if they were back East, living in relative comfort, he might just think about courting the young woman. But he wouldn't be thinking another such foolish thought. Two months, he decided. She wouldn't last a day longer than that. Too many challenges. Like… "How did she manage the Schmidt boys?"

The family had been in the community only a few months. John, the father, could barely make himself understood and he knew Mrs. Schmidt spoke not one word of English.

"Miss White taught them lots already. She said we must all help them. When George said he didn't come to play mama to some foreigner, Miss White said she would tolerate no unkindness."

Conor grunted. He knew George Crome. A big lad. It surprised him George's father hadn't kept him home to help with harvest, but then the Cromes weren't exactly suited to farming. They seemed to think the work would take care of itself. He imagined the way George would lift his nose and sniff at having to help two small boys. "What did George do?"

"At first he growled but Miss White reminded us we are all newcomers. Wouldn't we want people to help us?"

Sounded like a smart woman.

They neared the Faulks' property and a big brute of a dog raced toward them, barking and snarling. "I see Devin is visiting his folks." The dog belonged to the grown Faulk boy who wandered in and out at will. Conor turned the horse to face the dog and shouted, "Stop. Go back."

The dog halted, his hackles raised, his lips rolled back to reveal his vicious teeth. But he didn't advance.

Rae's fist clutched at his shirt as if she thought the horse would rear and she might fall.

"Noble isn't about to let an old dog make him act crazy."

Her fingers uncurled. "Yeah, I know." She sounded a little uncertain.

"You aren't scared of that old dog, are ya?"

"Nah."

"Good, because he's nothing but hot air and bluff."

They resumed their journey and his thoughts slid uninvited and unwelcome back to the schoolmarm. Rae's mind must have made the same journey because she resumed talking about the day.

"Miss White asked George what his best subject was. He's very good at arithmetic. Miss White gave him all sorts of problems to solve and he did them all. Miss White said he needed to cap'lize on his strengths. Pa, what does cap'lize mean?"

He grinned, picturing little Miss White finding a way to make George feel good after a scolding.

"Capitalize means to make the most of something."

"I like Miss White." Rae's voice was soft, filled with awe.

Conor's skin prickled. He knew his little daughter missed having a mother. But she would only be hurt if she looked for a substitute.

"I hope she stays."

Best to make Rae face the truth. But he wanted to spare her pain. Maybe with a little help she would figure it out herself. "You think she will?"

"She's smart."

"Uh-huh. But is she tough?"

"She's awfully pretty."

He squeezed the reins until they dug into his palm. He'd endured enough pain and disappointment with pretty women. So had Rae. Best she face facts and deal with them. "Now, Rae, how many times have I told you what use is pretty?"

"Yeah, Pa. I know. A person has to be strong to survive."

"Don't you be forgetting it." They turned toward their little house. This was where they belonged. He would fight to keep this place. He'd teach Rae to deal with the hardships. "You go on in while I unsaddle Noble."

A few minutes later he returned to the house, intent on getting a drink of water before he resumed working. Rae stood peering into the cracked mirror over the washstand. She turned as she heard him enter and grinned, waiting for him to admire her hair.

He felt like someone whacked him alongside the head with a big old plank. Oh, how she looked like her mother. "Hair ribbons." Pretty stuff. Useless stuff. The sort of thing that made women pine for a life that wasn't possible out here. People—men and women alike and children, too—had to forget the ease of life back East where supplies were around the corner, help and company across the fence and being pretty and stylish mattered. Out here survival mattered and woe to anyone who forgot. Or pined for things to be different. His wife had done the latter. She'd willingly left the comfort of Kansas City to follow his dream of owning land but she'd been unprepared for the challenges. In the end, she'd let them defeat her. She got a cold that turned fatal because she didn't have the will to live. "Where did you get them?" His mouth felt gritty.

"Miss White gave them to me. And Hilda did my hair." Her eyes were awash with hope and longing.

He could allow this tiny bit of joy. But no. He must not allow weakness in himself any more than he could allow it in Rae. "Tomorrow we give them back."

"Pa." Pleading made her drag out the syllable.

"How many times have I told you? Only the strong survive out here. You want to survive or don't you?"

"Yes, Pa."

"You and me are going to make ourselves a home out here. Now aren't we?"

"That's right, Pa."

"Then put the ribbons aside before they get dirty and tend to your chores."

She nodded. In her eyes determination replaced hope. And how that hurt him. But he had to be strong for the both of them. She pulled off the ribbons, rolled them neatly and put them beside her lunch bucket.

"There's hours of daylight left. I've got to get the crop cut and stooked. Uncle Gabe will be coming any day." He and Gabe helped each other. "I won't be back until dark. You know what to do. Think you can handle it?"

She tossed him a scoffing look. "I can handle it. You know it."

He pulled her against his hip for a quick hug. "Proud of you, Rae."

"You'll come in and say good night when you get home? Even if I'm sleeping."

"Always. You can see me from the yard. If you need me all you have to do is bang on the old barrel."

"I know."

He hated to leave her although he'd been doing so longer than he cared to think about. Since Irene had laid down and quit living more than two years ago, leaving him to raise Rae on his own. But he didn't have much choice. The work did not do itself, contrary to the hopes of men such as Mr. Crome.

He turned and headed for the field as Rae went to gather eggs.

It was dark when he returned. He searched the kitchen for something to eat and settled for a jam sandwich. He wiped dried jam from a knife in order to use it. They were about out of dishes fit to eat

from. He'd have to see if Rae would wash a few.
He'd also have to find time to go see Mrs. Jones
who sold him his weekly supply of bread.

Rae had dumped out her lunch bucket in preparation for tomorrow's food. The hair ribbons lay on
the lid.

Miss White would no doubt look all distressed
when he returned the ribbons and set her straight
about what was best for Rae. He could imagine her
floundering as she tried to apologize. Best she learn
life here was tough.

Maybe she could return to her safe home back
wherever she'd come from. Before she had to endure
the harshness of a Dakota winter.

Yet he felt no satisfaction at knowing he would
be among those who drove Miss White away. And
his regret made him want to kick himself seven
ways to Sunday. He knew better than most the folly
of subjecting a pretty woman to the barren pioneer
life.

He checked on Rae. She slept in her shirt, her
overalls bunched up on the floor beside the bed.
Dirty clothes lay scattered across the floor. He didn't
have time to do laundry until after harvest.

He pulled the covers around Rae and stood
watching her for a few minutes. He would never
understand how Irene could give up on life. He
thought she shared his goal. Having grown up in
Kansas City with a father who went from one job

to another and took the family from one poor hovel to the next, he'd vowed to provide for himself and his family a safe, permanent home even if he had to wrench it from this reluctant land with his bare fists. He would let nothing stand in his way. Not weakness. Certainly not a hankering after silly, useless, pretty things. Rae's mother should have fought. For Rae if not other reasons. He renewed his daily vow to make sure Rae had a safe and permanent home.

Chapter Two

He took Rae to school the next day. "Run and tell Miss White I need to speak to her, then go play with your friends." He didn't want Rae hearing this conversation.

Miss White paused to speak to one of the Schmidt boys as she crossed the yard to where he waited. She smiled at him as she drew closer. Her lips were pressed together. No flash of white teeth like he'd seen as she spoke to the children. Perhaps Rae had said something to warn her of his displeasure.

He held out his hand. "Here's your hair ribbons."

She refused to lift her hand and take them. "I gave them to Rachael. They're hers."

"She has no need of them. This is pioneer country. One has to be strong to survive."

"And how, sir, does a ribbon in one's hair make

for weakness. Does it somehow suck life blood out the roots of one's hair?" She faced him squarely, her eyes bold and challenging.

What happened to the apologetic distressed female he'd imagined? "It's what it signifies."

"You mean self-respect?"

She was one argumentative woman. "Useless things. Things for looks."

"Beauty is not a useless thing. It's a refreshing thing. Like a rainbow, a sunset or a blossom."

Conor wondered what use a blossom was. "Do any of those put food on the table or hay in the barn?"

"'Man shall not live by bread alone.'"

"Might surprise you to know that I recognize that as a Bible verse and I'm pretty sure it refers to needing God's word. It has nothing to do with things just for lookee see." He grabbed her hand and pulled it forward. He uncurled her fingers and pushed the ribbons into her fist. "Don't have no need for hair ribbons."

My how her eyes did flash, as full of fire as a winter stove. Faint color brushed her cheeks, making her look like some kind of fine china. But the way she stood, her fists clenched at her side and her jaw jutted out as if about to challenge him to defend himself, he knew she was a little scrapper. He liked that in a person.

His thoughts collided so harshly he reached for

his forehead intending to grab it to stop the sudden headache, but then he thought better of it. No way would he let her guess she'd surprised him.

Yeah, she might fight for an ideal while surrounded by safety of the schoolyard, a town within walking distance and a home in one of the finest houses in the virgin settlement. But real life was vastly different. "Pretty little hair ribbons and righteous indignation are about as necessary and helpful as…" His thoughts stalled. "As dandelion fluff."

She sniffed and tossed her head as if his words were meaningless. "Are you going to tell God His creation is useless?" She stomped away—daintily, of course—without a backward look.

Which left him no choice but to call to her back. "Me and Rae are survivors."

Survivors! As if that provided excuse enough for the way he treated Rachael. Forcing her to grow up like a boy. Virnie paused inside the door where no one could see her and struggled to gain control of her emotions.

Miss Price had helped her get past the feelings deposited by her father.

She lifted her head. She would do the same for Rachael. There were things she could do in school and she intended to do them but she'd like to help the girl more.

Lord God, provide me an opportunity.

* * *

The next two days Conor brought Rachael to school and returned to wait for her when the day ended. He didn't ride away until Virnie looked at him. And his look warned her not to interfere with the way he raised his daughter.

His silent insistence only increased her determination. She *would* find a way to help Rachael. She continued to pray for some kind of opening.

Friday afternoon, the children raced home, happy for the weekend. Except for Rachael who sat on a swing outside, waiting for her father.

Virnie, having no desire to see Conor again and relive all the emotions that insisted on surfacing each time she saw him, remained at her desk marking papers. Or at least she tried. Finally she put her pencil down, planted her elbows on the ink-stained surface and tipped her head into her palms. It was seven years since she last saw her father. She'd firmly put that part of her life behind her when she left with Miss Price. It was dead and gone as far as she was concerned. So why did it haunt her?

She sighed and returned to marking the papers. She knew Conor was the reason. Conor and Rachael. Their situation too clearly mirrored her early life and brought back unwanted memories.

The swing creaked. Virnie glanced out the window. Rachael still waited. Where was her father? She moved to the window and glanced down the road. No sign of dust indicating a rider. She slipped out to join the girl, sitting on the nearby swing so they could talk.

"Is your Pa coming for you?"

Rachael scuffed her shoes in the dust and studied the tracks she made. "Don't think so."

"How are you to get home?"

"Walk. Done it lots of times."

Virnie waited, wondering why the child hadn't already left but Rachael didn't seem about to offer any answers. "Did you want something?" Perhaps this was the opening she'd prayed for. "Is your father at home?"

"He's cutting the crop."

"I see." Only it didn't answer her question as to whether or not he would be watching for her return. "Do you want to help me clean the chalkboard?"

"Sure." She raced back to the school, Virnie on her heels. As they washed the board and cleaned the brushes, Virnie talked and silently prayed.

"I sure appreciate your help. You're a good worker."

"Pa says a person has to pull their weight in this country."

Virnie supposed it was true about most places. She wanted to know how Rachael felt about being a girl. "Guess it doesn't matter if you're a boy or a girl, you can do your share."

"Pa says women have to be strong in order

to survive out here. Say there's no room for weakness."

He did, did he? Well, strength could be disguised under velvet just as much as it could be revealed in leather. And it was time Conor found that out. Except she didn't plan to be the person to show him. He reminded her too much of her past and she didn't welcome the reminder.

She washed the chalk dust off her hands. "The blackboard and brushes are nice and clean, ready for Monday morning."

Rachael had no reason to linger and yet she did. Tiny bubbles of apprehension skittered along Virnie's nerves and she shivered. Was there a reason Rachael did not want to go home? Was Conor hurting her physically and Rachael wanted to tell Virnie but didn't know how? "Is there something wrong at home that you don't want to go there?"

Rachael shot her a surprised look. "Not at home."

Relief warmed Virnie's veins. Somehow she found it difficult to contemplate an abusive Conor. "Then what's wrong?"

Rachael hung her head and studied her toes.

Virnie caught the girl's chin and forced her to face Virnie. She kept her voice soft even though tension made her feel brittle inside. "Tell me what's wrong."

Rachael scrubbed her lips together as she

considered Virnie. Finally, her dark brown eyes wide, she whispered, "I don't want to walk home."

"But why? Haven't you done it lots of times before?"

Rachael shrugged and pulled away. "It's nothing."

"No. Something is bothering you. Tell me what it is and maybe I can help."

"You can't do nothing."

She ignored the poor grammar. "Why don't you let me decide that?"

Rachael shuddered. "It's Faulks' dog." The child's fear beat like something alive.

But Virnie wasn't getting any closer to what bothered Rachael. "Who are the Faulks?"

"They live on my way home."

"Ahh. So you pass their place and you're afraid of the dog?"

Rachael shot her head up and gave Virnie a defiant look. "I'm not scared." But her eyes said she was.

Virnie made up her mind to see if the fear was legitimate or not. But she sensed she would offend Rachael if she made her plan obvious. "Rachael, I'm planning to visit all of my students' homes. This afternoon would be a good time for me to visit you. Would you mind if I walk home with you?"

Tension drained out of the child so quickly she swayed. "That would be nice."

Virnie closed the windows and the door then followed Rachael outside. They walked along the dusty road. The day was warm with a breeze that kept it from being unbearable. The sky was so blue that if Virnie lifted her head she could feel like she walked into a vast flat lake. Birds lifted from the yellow blades of grass as they passed, calling out a warning as they flew away.

Rachael skipped along beside her, chattering about all sorts of things until they had gone a mile and she slowed drastically. A house stood on a rise of land a few hundred feet away.

Virnie made a few quick assumptions. "This must be where the Faulks live."

"Shh. If we're really quiet maybe the dog won't hear us." Rachael tiptoed at the far edge of the road.

Virnie abandoned the middle of the road in favor of the side as well, not sure what she faced but certain of Rachael's fear. Surely, she consoled herself, no one would keep a dog that threatened a child. Surely, Rachael's fears were unfounded.

A snarling black shape bowled toward them.

Virnie's heart clamored up her throat. This was the dog Rachael feared and for good reason. He barreled toward them like a freight train. Virnie backed away, her mouth suddenly as dry as the dust at their feet.

Rachael grabbed Virnie's skirt and pressed close to her back. "It's him. He's going to get us."

Something fierce and hot surged through Virnie. "No, he's not." She faced the attacking dog, now within twenty feet of the road. "Stop," she yelled with all the authority she could muster. "Stop."

The dog didn't slow down one iota.

"Don't move," she told Rachael though she wondered if either of them could force their limbs to run.

She lowered her voice to her deepest tones. "Stop."

A distant voice called, "Tictoc, you get back here right now, hear."

The dog slowed slightly.

Virnie tore her gaze from the approaching menace to the house. A plump woman stood on the step waving a broom.

"Tictoc, don't you make me come after you." The woman banged the broom against the wall.

The dog stopped, still growling, still considering whether he wanted to continue his attack or obey the cross mistress.

"Tictoc, I'm warning you. Get back here. Now." Another solid whack with the broom.

The dog edged backward, clearly wanting to complete what he had started. But another whack of the broom made him turn and slink away. Virnie stared as he skittered past the house and disappeared under a nearby fence.

The danger was over but she couldn't move. Couldn't speak. Her lungs seemed to have forgotten their job was to provide oxygen to her body. Her brain remained in shocked numbness.

"He's gone," Rachael whispered. "Let's go."

Virnie's breath escaped in a loud whoosh and she leaned forward as she sucked in air. She must not let Rachael know how frightened she'd been. Sudden anger pushed her fear into distant corners. "Does that dog threaten you every time you walk by?"

"If he's here. He belongs to Devin Faulk. He's their son. He has a farm south of here and takes the dog with him. I like it when he's not here."

Virnie started to giggle. She knew it was a mixture of relief and anger. "Tictoc? What sort of name is that for a dog?" She tried to control her giggles but couldn't.

Rachael stared at her and blinked, then her eyes sparkled. "Tictoc like a clock." For some reason the little rhyme amused them both immensely and they giggled like mad.

They continued toward the Russell home.

"That's my house," Rachael said with obvious pride, pausing to let Virnie have a good look.

Virnie saw a low house of moderate size and felt an instant sense of relief. At least Rachael didn't live in one of those tarpaper shacks some of the settlers had for a dwelling, nor in a sod shanty. The wood had not been painted but it looked a substantial enough place. To one side were pens for the animals and a sod-roofed building she took for the barn. A small pen housed chickens and another fenced area indicated what might have been a garden. Some buckets lay scattered along the garden fence. Rags were caught along another fence. Apart from the general air of untidiness, it seemed to promise a solid future. Virnie stood several minutes taking it all in, trying to confine her feelings to how this affected Rachael but she couldn't stop a trickle of memories. She enjoyed hours with her brother, Miles, at a farm. One bigger and more developed than this one, but seeing the pens and the barn brought things to mind she'd purposely pushed away. Following Miles around, trying to imitate him, trying to earn his approval, hoping if she did, her father would voice his…what? She didn't know what she'd expected then any more than she did now. Perhaps a word of praise, a sign that he didn't regret having a daughter? She turned from studying the Russell farm. "Are you going to show me your house?"

Rachael grabbed her hand and ran. Virnie had no choice but to trot after her.

They ducked into the house. Virnie remembered her manners in time to stifle a gasp at the mess before her. They stood in a nice-sized room that served as living quarters for the residents—combining sitting area, dining area and kitchen. The room had potential to be bright and cheerful but it did not live up to its possibilities. Dirty dishes covered the table. The stove held an array of blackened pots and pans. Clothing of every description from a Rachael-sized shirt to a heavy winter coat lay scattered across every surface. Virnie had to wonder where they sat, how they managed to prepare a meal, how they kept clean. She deliberately shifted her gaze to the two doors opening into the room. Both stood open to reveal beds buried beneath clothing and assorted objects. How did they find room to sleep in those beds? And how did Rachael manage to find clean clothes to wear to school?

Mentally, Virnie began to roll up her sleeves. She could tackle the worst of this mess while she was here, perhaps show Rachael a few coping skills. She wondered how long she had until Conor returned because she didn't have to be a genius to sense he would object to her interference.

"Rae." The faint call came from outside, some distance away.

Rachael grabbed Virnie's hand. "Don't tell Pa about the dog."

The child's request drove all else from Virnie's mind. She assumed it would be the first thing Rachael said. Such an encounter should be reported and dealt with. Why was Rachael afraid to tell

Conor? "You need to let him know so he can do something."

"No. Pa needs me to be strong."

"Rachael, you need to be protected."

Rachael swallowed so hard she grimaced. "I can take care of myself."

Virnie knew she couldn't. What if Mrs. Faulk hadn't been there to call the dog off? Virnie shuddered to think of the child facing that dog alone. "You need to tell him."

Rachael shook her head. "Promise you won't tell."

Virnie considered her responsibility to report the incident against the child's obvious reluctance. "I won't tell him but I want you to promise you will. He needs to know."

"Okay, I will." Her reluctance was obvious.

Conor burst into the house and Virnie could not pursue the subject. She had given her word. Now she must trust Rachael to keep hers.

"Where have you been? Why are you so late?" Conor demanded of Rachael and then he shifted his gaze to Virnie. "Why did you bring her home?"

"Pa, she is visiting all the families and I got to be first."

Conor narrowed his eyes, still studying Virnie. "Is that a fact?"

Virnie's struggle to deal with her reluctant promise about the dog ended suddenly at the challenge in his voice.

"Do you have any objections?" She meant both visiting in general and making Rachael her first visit.

He blinked before her directness. "Why is Rae so late?"

"She helped me clean the chalkboard and brushes so we could walk home together." She darted a glance at Rachael, hoping to convey that now would be a good time to tell her father about the dog. But Rachael refused to meet her eyes.

"Do you expect me to serve you tea?"

She almost laughed but managed to confine her amusement to a grin. "I'm not sure that would be a good idea." She let her gaze circle the room and knew a sense of victory when he looked uncomfortable.

"It's harvest time. Don't have time to spend cleaning up the house. It can wait. The crops can't."

She didn't say it looked like the house had waited a very long time but knew her eyes must have flashed her disbelief when he scowled.

The sound of an approaching rider reached them.

"It's Uncle Gabe," Conor said.

Rachael screamed and raced outside calling, "Uncle Gabe. Uncle Gabe."

Conor did not release Virnie from his look, rife with warning, but beneath that she read more—his latent worry about Rachael being late. Realizing his unspoken concern, something sharp and hot drove through her thoughts. This man cared about his daughter even though he treated her like a boy. Perhaps she could appeal to him on that basis, somehow make him see the harm he inadvertently inflicted on his child. She could explain—but pain twisted through her at the mere thought of telling someone how it felt.

The look in his blue, bottomless eyes shifted, seeking a response that had nothing to do with Rachael.

A noise outside made him jerk toward the door, freeing her from his stare and allowing her to think clearly. She didn't intend to get involved with this man. Yes, he might care in a flawed way about his daughter but Virnie did not have any desire to relive her own experience in order to help him. She would pray for some other way to help Rachael.

"I've been expecting him," Conor said.

"Your brother?" Virnie asked.

"No, just a good friend."

"I'll be on my way." But before Virnie could make her way through the door, Rachael returned, pulling a man by his hand.

His eyes widened when he saw her and he whipped off his hat. "Didn't know Conor had a lady friend visiting." He grinned widely at Conor then shifted his attention back to Virnie. He didn't say anything but the way his grin deepened, Virnie knew he thought she was worth a second look.

She took the liberty of giving him a good look, too. A man with fine features, blond hair, blue eyes and unrepentant amusement.

"'Bout time old Conor acknowledged there's more to life than work."

Conor grunted. "Miss White is the new schoolteacher." He nodded toward Virnie. "You probably figured out this is my friend, Gabe. Gabe Winston."

"Pleased to meet you, ma'am. And might you have a Christian name?"

"Virnie." She looked at Conor as she spoke, wondering if he would ever take the liberty of using her name. But he scowled like he had a pain somewhere. She pulled herself straighter. She knew that look. Had seen it often from her pa. And she understood she was the source of the pain. For Conor as well as her pa. "I'll be on my way. Good day."

Gabe made a protesting noise but stepped aside as she steamed out.

She hurried away with long, furious strides. Why did she let Conor's attitude pull unwanted memories to her mind?

She stomped hard on the dusty surface of the road, raising dust to her knees. She'd have to polish her shoes and brush her skirt when she got home.

The extra emphasis to each step did nothing to stop her from remembering.

Too bad you're a girl.

After all this time, the words still twisted her heart into an agonized knot.

Lord God, the past is past. You provided Miss Price to give me a different life. Help me forget those days of pain and uncertainty.

Her thoughts slipped to Rachael. How similar their situations. If Miss Price were here she'd surely find a way to help. What would she do?

Virnie stopped at the school to get some papers and texts so she could prepare lessons then returned to Maxwell house where she boarded. She liked living with them. Their formal parlor and old-fashioned furniture reminded her of living with Miss Price. She found comfort in their routine and stiff mannerisms that also reminded her of Miss Price. She paused to greet Mrs. Maxwell then retired to her bedroom to pen a letter to Miss Price. In great detail she told about her first week, asking advice on how to teach the Schmidt boys English and how to challenge young George to apply as much interest to literature and penmanship as he did to arithmetic.

She closed with, "There is a child who reminds me of myself. She is motherless. Her father dresses her like a boy. He expects her to be tough. I would like to help her but find myself dealing with memories of my own past that I prefer to ignore. I must in all honesty say this child's father doesn't seem to be unkind toward her."

Thinking of Conor filled her with confusion. Her first glimpse of him convinced her he cared about Rachael. Today she knew she'd seen worry in his eyes over Rachael's tardiness in returning from school. She'd seen something in him that made her lonesome inside. But when had she become so maudlin? She had only to consider Rachael's fear about the Faulks' dog to know there was something wrong.

She turned back to her letter. "Please pray that I might have wisdom in this situation." What if God wanted her to do more like Miss Price had done? "And the courage to do what needs to be done."

Chapter Three

Gabe stared after Miss White and as soon as she was out of earshot, let out a low whistle. "You sure know how to pick 'em."

Conor snorted. "She's Rae's teacher. I had nothing to do with her being hired." His insides had gradually grown tenser as he watched for Rae to return from school and when he'd seen Miss White escorting her, all he could think was Rae had been hurt. He'd crossed the field in great leaps. To discover Miss White only wanted to check on him had only twisted his insides further because of the strange mix of unwanted emotions—embarrassment at the state of his house, defensiveness at her silent accusation and—he didn't want to acknowledge it but he couldn't deny it—*loneliness*. He'd had a sudden flash of what life could be like with a woman to share the load.

Even now he kicked himself mentally at his nonsense. He'd learned the pain of expecting a beautiful, gentle woman to accept frontier life. He dreamed that dream and reaped the disappointment and grief. A lesson he didn't intend to repeat. He'd ask for and expect help from neither God nor man—or perhaps he meant it was only from women he couldn't expect help.

Not that he'd lost his belief in God. Just his trust.

"Being a teacher don't make her less pretty." Gabe poked him in the ribs to emphasize his point.

Rae hung from Gabe's arm. "I told Pa she was pretty, too."

Conor shot them both a look burning with fury. "Tell me what good pretty is." He strode out the door. Of course it was too much to expect Gabe would take the hint and shut up on the matter.

"Pretty is mighty nice to see when a man returns home tired and hungry."

Conor put up mental barriers at Gabe's reminder of what he missed. "I suppose you count yourself an expert? Don't see you inviting young Diana to join you." Gabe had left his intended back in Philadelphia when he came West promising to send for her when he was settled. That was two years ago.

"Figure it's about time. Soon as I get the barn up and the harvest in."

Conor scoffed. "Heard that last year."

"My barn's still not up."

"We'll do that this fall." He figured mentioning that fact would give Gabe something to think about. Seems he came up with more excuses than necessary for not sending for Diana. Conor kind of figured Gabe wasn't quite ready to commit to marriage. He guessed the delay wasn't a bad idea and wanted to warn Gabe that Diana might have unreal expectations about what pioneering meant but didn't want to turn the conversation back to the one topic he wished to avoid—the risk of expecting a woman to labor at his side. Gabe's side, he corrected.

"So what was Virnie doing out here? Seems a long way from the schoolhouse."

"Miss White—" he emphasized the proper title "—seems to think she should visit each of her students' homes."

He felt Gabe's amused grin directed at him but ignored it and tromped toward the field where the last of the sheaves waited to be stoked. "Rae, you look after your chores."

"Yes, Pa." She dropped back, disappointed at missing out on the conversation.

Gabe waved to her. "See you later, little gal." He closed the distance between himself and Conor. "So how many other homes has Virnie visited, do you suppose?"

"I'd guess none."

"Mighty interesting that she chooses this place first."

Conor stopped and faced his friend. "I know what you're doing. But I am not interested in Miss White. You saw her. Does she look the type to embrace frontier life?"

Gabe shrugged. "She came of her own free will, one would assume."

"And I expect she will leave of her own free will before Christmas."

"Conor, not every woman is like Irene. Some are even stronger than their men. Why, you only have to look down the road to the Faulks. It's the old lady who does most of the work while the mister supervises and her son wanders about looking for who knows what. Sure, he says he has a farm somewhere but I have my doubts."

His example supported Conor's argument. "When was the last time you had a good look at Mrs. Faulk? She's built like a small ox. Nothing pretty or soft about her."

Gabe laughed loudly. "I bet all that padding's plenty soft."

"You know what I mean."

Gabe stopped and faced him, forcing Conor to stop, too, or reveal his dislike of this conversation by ducking around him. He chose to face the man squarely.

"I know what you mean better than you do." Gabe seemed intent on speaking his mind.

"Humph."

"Yup, you're scared you might get hurt again. I've said it before and I'll say it again. Not all women are like Irene."

Conor refrained from voicing a warning that Gabe might soon enough discover for himself the true facts of the situation. "Look, are we going to stand around jawing all day or get this crop harvested? Could be you're delaying so you don't have to send for Diana."

"I guess I'll have to prove you wrong." He bent his back and worked like this was the last day available.

The next two days Rae teased Gabe into giving her a ride to school and picking her up afterward. It interrupted their workday and made Conor uneasy. Sure, Rae liked Gabe's attention but was this something else? He began to suspect Miss White had said or done something to make Rae think she must be escorted to school. On the third morning, he decided to test his theory.

"Rae, Gabe's too busy to take you to school. You'll have to walk. Same after school."

"Okay, Pa." She skipped off down the road.

Conor stared after her. There went that suspicion and with it the argument he'd used to deflect the memory of Miss White standing in this very room.

Gabe, as always honing in on his secret thoughts, punched him on the shoulder. "If you didn't want me seeing Virnie every morning you only had to say so or take Rae yourself."

Conor grabbed his hat. "Come on, let's get to work."

Several days later they worked on the last of Conor's crop. He enjoyed the hard work. It kept him from thinking too deeply about anything but the grain, the cows and his plans for the fall. Like Virnie White. It seemed everything he said or did made him think of her.

"I warned Diana how cold Dakota winters can be and she says she will bring lots of warm clothes and make some extra warm quilts."

If Gabe brought Diana out right after harvest, the two of them would share the cold winter months. Conor straightened and let his gaze rest on the house across the field. His house. His lonely house. When he'd moved West he had envisioned a home full of warmth and welcome. A flash of Virnie's pretty smiling face flitted across his mind. He blinked and dismissed it. He wasn't lonely enough for the kind of pain brought by sharing his life with a pretty woman.

Gabe watched him. "Virnie seems like a fine woman. I saw how she handles the kids. A fine woman, indeed. Perhaps you should get to know her better."

Conor didn't answer but he tossed bundles to Gabe fast enough to make him pant.

That night they scrounged a meal by opening several cans. They gave three plates a quick wipe and found a place to set them by pushing things off the table.

Conor saw the knowing look in Gabe's eyes and silently dared him to mention the state of the house and suggest it needed the touch of a woman. "Now my crop is done I'll make arrangements for Rae then we'll go to your place."

After they'd finished their simple meal, he rode over to the Joneses' where he normally left Rae if he planned to be gone overnight. They lived close enough Rae could run back and forth to look after the cows and the chickens. But Mrs. Jones was down with something and said she couldn't manage.

He returned home with the awkward news. "Can't take her with us. She needs to tend to the chores."

Rae edged forward. "You could get someone to stay here."

Something about the look on her face warned Conor her suggestion wouldn't be to his liking. "Maybe. But most everyone has chores at home."

"I know someone who doesn't have chores. Miss White."

"No." The word exploded from him.

Gabe chuckled. "You sound mighty scared and you won't even be here."

Conor did not want to picture her in his house, touching his belongings, filling his kettle, sweeping his floor. "No."

Gabe laughed hard. "Man, what's gotten into you? You're jumpy as a spring colt. Virnie must really have gotten under your collar."

"You can't begin to understand. And her name is Miss White."

"Ain't what she told me."

Conor knew an incredible urge to physically remove that teasing grin from Gabe's face.

Gabe leaned closer, making it even more tempting. "Seems to me you're overreacting, unless…" He dragged his sentence out as he sat back waving a finger. "You're more interested in her than you're willing to admit."

"You're plumb loco."

"Then ask her."

"Please, Pa, please."

Conor sighed loudly, letting the pair know just how annoying they were. "Fine. I'll ask. But don't expect she'll say yes."

Virnie had been grateful to Conor's friend for bringing Rachael to and from school. But it only lasted a few days. When Virnie got a chance to speak to Rachael privately, she learned the Faulk boy or man, whichever he was, had left again and taken the dog with him.

"Did you tell your pa about the dog?"

"Didn't need to. He's gone."

"What about when he comes back?"

Rachael gave an unconcerned shrug. "Maybe he won't." And Virnie had to be content with that. So why did she stare down the road every morning until Rachael arrived and check every afternoon, sighing in disappointment when Rachael marched down the road, swinging her lunch pail and kicking up little clouds of dust? It wasn't because she hoped Conor would ride up for his daughter. It couldn't be. Because she wouldn't allow herself such silly thoughts. His behavior was too much like her father's. And forget the worry and concern she'd seen in his face over Rachael. It didn't count.

And forget the way his probing look had stirred such an unfamiliar response deep inside in places she had never known existed. Now those places refused to be ignored despite her firmest efforts. The ignited feeling both frightened and thrilled her. With a decided shake of her head, she pulled her thoughts into submission and focused on the letter from Miss Price.

She skimmed over the suggestions on ways to help the Schmidt boys learn English more quickly and nodded as she hurried through the problems Miss Price had sent that would require George to do extra reading before he could solve the challenging arithmetic problems. She found what she really wanted at the end.

> As to your questions about your little student, bear in mind that not all parents are willing to let their children benefit from personal involvement with a teacher. In my experience, there has only been you and Belle.

Belle had been a student before Virnie. She came from a large family and when her parents decided to move farther west they made the choice to let Belle continue her education. Boarding with Miss Price had been a perfect solution for Belle. Her parents had left her reluctantly.

Unlike Virnie. In her case, she had learned to accept that her father was glad to be rid of her.

She turned back to the letter.

"That is not to say there aren't other ways of helping this child both inside and outside the classroom." Miss Price went on to list several scenarios such as involving Rachael in extra reading, or performing in a drama or being involved in some community endeavor. "I will pray for such opportunities."

Virnie folded the letter and put it in the drawer with the previous letters from Miss Price. She owed it to her mentor to do something for Rachael even if it meant having to deal with Conor and her errant feelings around him.

But what?

God would have to provide the answer.

The next day, Conor surprised her by bringing Rachael to school. Rachael ran to Virnie. "Pa wants to talk to you."

She wondered at the excitement in Rachael's voice. But her main concern when she crossed the yard to where Conor waited was controlling the sudden roll of her heart that left her breathless.

"You wanted to speak to me?" She kept her voice admirably calm despite the way her insides vibrated at speaking to this man who had inadvertently opened up an unwelcome door in her heart. She didn't know what lay past that open door and didn't intend to find out. She had her life plans laid out firmly. She would be a dedicated teacher such as Miss Price had trained her to be. And because it was what she wanted.

Conor seemed very interested in the reins draped across his palm. "Umm. I have to go to Gabe's farm and help him with his harvest."

She nodded. "Does that mean yours is done?"

"Yes, and a fair harvest, too."

"Good. I'm glad for you." Though she wondered what it had to do with her and why he continued to twist the reins.

"Rae can't go with me."

"Of course not. She has to attend school."

"And do the chores at home."

She nodded. "You'll miss her, I suppose." She had to see his response, assure herself he did care, that Rachael being a girl wasn't reason enough to resent her.

Conor's gaze rested on Rachael standing near the school watching them. Then he turned to look hard at Virnie.

She saw his stark feelings about his daughter. He loved her so much it seemed to almost hurt him.

"I will miss her." His voice was low, edged with roughness. "But out here we do what has to be done without complaining."

She nodded, not understanding the warning note in his voice.

He sucked in air and jerked his gaze away as if aware of the tension lacing the air between them. "She needs someone to stay with her."

"Certainly she does."

He shifted back to look at her. "Would you?"

His gaze was so intent, so demanding, she found it difficult to think. "Would I what?"

"Would you stay with her?"

Her mouth fell open. She forced it shut and swallowed hard. Was this God's answer for a way to spend more time with Rachael? He'd certainly found a unique way of doing it.

Conor took her hesitation for regret. "I wouldn't be there. Be gone for a week or two."

"Why I'd love to stay with her. On one condition."

His eyes narrowed. "Tell me before I agree."

"You allow me to teach her a few skills around the house."

Darkness filled his eyes. "Don't need fancy stuff."

"Seems to me from the little I saw that you would benefit from someone knowing a few basics like washing dishes and tidying up."

They did silent battle with their eyes and then he nodded. "So long as you don't teach her to be a silly, weak female."

She laughed, despite feeling like her past had slapped her full-on. "Female doesn't necessarily equate weak and silly." She'd tried to prove it to her father. Unfortunately, she had failed so miserably he had sent her away and never again contacted her. She pushed the hurt of her former life back into the shadows. This was not about her. It was about Rachael.

Conor only quirked his eyebrows at her quick defense. "I have to leave immediately. Take good care of her." He waved Rachael over.

Rachael raced to his side, darting cautious glances at Virnie. "She's going to do it?"

Conor nodded.

Virnie thought he looked like he regretted it already. She left them to say goodbye. But as she walked away she overhead him say, "Don't expect her to stay when things get hard."

Virnie grinned. If he thought she'd turn tail and run at the first challenge she encountered, he didn't know the things she'd faced in the past.

Chapter Four

Virnie found lots of work to do in the house and enlisted Rachael's help, hoping to teach her a few coping skills. Her first task was to wash dishes. It was a standard kind of job that occurred in every house across the nation every day. Only this was Conor's kitchen and as she scraped the dirty dishes she got glimpses of what he ate, the meager sort of meals he endured and wondered how either he or Rachael survived. She felt his presence in every corner of the room. She wondered how he spent his evenings. Did he read? She saw little evidence of it though she didn't venture into his room. She tried not to think of him sitting over a cup of tea, wanting to share his day with someone.

She pushed aside an increasingly familiar awareness of the empty areas of her life. It would be nice to share stories of her day with someone. She scoffed at her silliness. If she wanted to share she had only to sit down and pen a letter to Miss Price. But it wasn't the same.

When Rachael complained they didn't need to wash all the dishes, only what they needed, Virnie chuckled. "Sounds like something your pa says."

"Yup." Then thinking Virnie might expect better English from her, corrected herself. "Yes. 'No need to waste time on needless chores,' he says."

Virnie tried to think of a way to show Rachael that house chores were as necessary as farm chores. "Why does your pa insist the pens are cleaned every day?"

"Easier to move a little manure than a lot."

"Same with dishes. It's easier to wash what you use every day than face the dirty stack when you run out."

Rachael looked startled.

"So we'll wash all these dishes and put them away and then every day you wash the ones you use. That way you don't have to try and find something clean when you're hungry."

They finished the stack. Virnie scrubbed the cupboard and put everything away. "Doesn't that look nice?" The tabletop was clean and scrubbed, the stove shiny black.

Rachael giggled. "Pa wouldn't know it was the same place."

They tackled the rest of the room. Virnie discovered beautiful wood floors that gleamed once she'd scrubbed and polished them. She saw Conor's handwork in the hand-hewn window ledges and his craftsmanship in every detail of the house. The house revealed a pride that belied its current condition. There must have been a time he valued a nice home.

As Virnie polished a window, she wondered what had caused Conor to change his mind. Certainly the death of his wife formed a large part of it. Aching for his loss, she pressed her lips together to stop their trembling.

Friday afternoon, she followed Rachael into the cleaned house and stopped as a wave of sensations poured over her again, making her feel teary. She struggled to identify the cause of her reaction. The place felt like home. She felt she had a part in making it welcome. It wasn't her home and never would be but a longing for such a home and welcome grabbed at her insides until she struggled to catch her breath.

She closed her eyes momentarily to stop the sensation.

This was not what she wanted. No. She had set her heart on being a teacher like Miss Price—helping many children, devoting herself to a worthy cause.

She gathered her thoughts and hung her hat on the nearby hook. Next to Conor's coat. His scent filled her senses—masculine, and hinting of his work with animals, reminiscent of her days helping Miles. She rested her head against the wall and fought for control. This was Conor and Rachael's home. Her home was a tiny room in the home of Mr. and Mrs. Maxwell. Miss Price had taught her to enjoy the privacy of her own room and to realize the rest of the house belonged to others. It was the way things were for teachers. Virnie knew it well and not only accepted it, she enjoyed it.

So why this sudden, overwhelming reaction to a house she had cleaned and polished, this blur of tears at the bouquet of scents from Conor's coat—reminding her both of Miles and Conor?

Rachael ran out to gather eggs then returned for the milk pail.

"Pa says I'm the best little milker. I can milk the cow faster than he can. I think it's 'cause she likes me."

She was gone again, leaving Virnie struggling with her war of emotions. She touched Conor's coat, fingering the woolen texture, freeing another waft of scents. Why did he treat Virnie like she couldn't be counted on? Why did he try and make Rachael so tough? What had happened to his wife?

She jerked her fingers from the fabric and pushed herself from the wall, away from her silly meanderings. It was the weekend and she intended to tackle

Rachael's room today. Tomorrow she would wash clothes.

As soon as Rachael returned and the milk was tended to, Virnie led the way to the bedroom. "Rachael, remember what I say in school? A neat desk is an efficient desk. Same with your bedroom. Keep it clean and you'll waste far less time looking for things."

Before they could put anything away, it was necessary to clean out the drawers of the chiffonier. In the bottom one, under a collection of rocks and feathers and other little treasures, Virnie found a picture.

"This must be your mother. You look very much like her." A beautiful woman with lovely hair.

Rachael grabbed the picture from Virnie's hands. "Don't tell Pa I got this. I'm supposed to forget her."

Virnie struggled to hide her shock. It hurt to forget one's mother. "Why is that?"

"Because she was weak. She was supposed to help him but Pa says she just lay down and quit living all because she missed the easy life of the city. Pa says we have to work hard to have a home no one can take from us."

That explained so much. His insistence that Rachael be tough, his neglect of the house—no doubt the poor man had lost his dreams along with his wife. Or did men *have* dreams?

Rachael put the picture back in the drawer and covered it with an old shirt. "I don't want to disobey Pa but I want to have a ma, too, even if it's only her picture."

"I understand. I won't tell your pa."

They worked together sorting out the room, but Virnie's thoughts tended to stray. She identified with Rachael's need for a mother. In Virnie's case, Miss Price had proved an adequate substitute. But a person needed a pa, too. Hers hadn't wanted her so she'd struggled to forget that need. But in spite of her sincerest attempts, she could not shake the desire for recognition from her father. Somehow, she had to make Rachael realize how fortunate she was to have that even if it carried a requirement to be tough.

"At least you have your pa and you know he cares about you."

Rachael giggled. "He loves me but says it might make me soft if he tells me. So he saves it for special occasions."

Virnie couldn't help wondering what occasions constituted as special enough for the words so she asked.

"Christmas morning, the first thing he says is, 'I love you, Rae.' And my birthday." Rachael giggled again. "He makes up special occasions, too—the first robin of spring, the first snowfall. Stuff like that."

Virnie's throat tightened and her teeth felt brittle. Tears threatened. As Miss Price often said, her eyes had a tendency to leak. But thinking of Conor's tenderness hidden under the cloak of his toughness touched her in secret places that ached for something she didn't dare identify. It so filled her with longing and wanting that she struggled to contain her emotions. If only she could have the same tenderness extended to her. Her imagination raced out of control. She saw herself standing in the living area she had recently cleaned, a savory meal simmering on the stove as she awaited Conor's return and a taste of that tenderness.

Chastising herself for her inability to rein in her thoughts, she grabbed an armload of dirty clothes off the bed. "Tomorrow you can help me do the laundry." Hooks on one wall burgeoned with more clothes. "Let's sort these out." She quickly determined many of the items were too small or needed serious repair. The last item on one hook was a pretty blue calico dress. Virnie held it out. "This looks new."

"It is. My grandma from Philadelphia sent it."

"Why don't you wear it?"

"I'd only get it dirty."

"It will wash."

"Overalls make more sense."

Virnie didn't pursue the topic knowing Rachael quoted her father but she had an idea.

Sunday morning, she approached her plan. "I attend church Sunday. I'd like you to come with me."

Rachael brightened at the idea. "Can I?"

"Of course. Let's get prettied up." She'd worn a simple cotton dress in demure gray with a lace-trimmed collar. She'd fashioned her hair into a loose chignon. "Why don't you wear that dress?"

Rachael shook her head. "Pa says I don't need to dress up to impress God. Says God's seen me before I was born and every day since and lots of times naked."

Virnie laughed. "That's true but I think putting on our best clothes for church shows God we respect Him. After all, we wouldn't go visit the president in anything but our best, would we?"

"I guess not."

"Then run and put on your dress."

Rachael headed toward her room with obvious reluctance. She emerged a few minutes later in the dress. The blue brought out her natural coloring.

"You look very nice." Virnie had one more chal-lenge. "I have some pretty hair ribbons that match that dress perfectly."

"Pa said we got no need for useless pretty things."

"I only thought they might keep your hair in place. Keep you tidy. But if you don't want to…" Virnie made as if to put the ribbons away.

Rachael's eyes followed Virnie's hands with obvious regret. "I guess it wouldn't hurt to be tidy. Seeing we're going to church."

Virnie hesitated. "You're sure?"

Rachael nodded. "I think Pa would agree they serve a useful purpose."

"Of course they do. Now sit on a chair while I tend to your hair." The child had thick wavy hair that required patience to brush. But Virnie didn't mind. She loved caring for this child, doing for her all the things Virnie had never had done. As she brushed Rachael's hair she wondered why she couldn't recall her mother. Virnie had been five when she died but she seemed to have disappeared from memory. In fact, until she met Rachael she had forgotten her father and Miles, too, except for brief, unwelcome flashes. Of course, Miss Price's counsel to put her past life behind her had caused Virnie to do her best to forget it. But she wished she had a picture of her mother like Rachael did. Somehow it would be comforting to have some reminder.

"There. You're done. Have a look."

Rachael went to the small mirror over the washstand and turned back and forth examining her reflection.

"What do you think?"

"It looks nice."

Virnie hugged her. "You look very pretty." Rachael stiffened a bit and Virnie guessed she thought of her father's words about pretty being useless for a pioneer. But he was wrong. A person— a woman—could be pretty, or at least pleasant- looking, and still face the challenges of this new land.

Monday after classes ended, Rachael hopped about as she waited for Virnie to close up the school. "Pa should be back tomorrow."

"How can you know?"

"'Cause the weather's been good. He said it would take seven days of good weather. He'll be back. He never stays away longer than he has to."

Rachael had such confidence in her father's affec- tion. "Shall we make it a special occasion?"

"How can we do that?"

"Well, you could help me make a special meal." She'd been able to fashion simple meals from the eggs, milk and a decent supply of canned goods. On Saturday, as she draped the wet clothes on the fence surrounding the garden patch, she'd found evidence of potatoes and carrots.

Rachael had explained, "Pa plants a garden every spring."

Virnie shook her head. Weeding the garden might actually allow them to reap some produce. But upon closer examination she unearthed useable potatoes and carrots. "Where does your pa get meat?"

"Goes to the store. I can go and Mr. Brown will

sell me something and put it on Pa's bill. I've done that before. Are we going to make a real meal?"

A real meal. For a real family. In a real home. The words danced through Virnie's mind like the taunt of teasing children. Or the echo of her own heart. "We'll get some meat on our way home tomorrow." She squeezed Rachael. "We'll cook a real meal." And then her sojourn into pretend would end and she'd return to her lifetime goal.

There was no reason she should dread the idea. None whatsoever.

Conor rode into the yard. Through the window, he glimpsed Rae and Virnie. He wanted to see Rae and assure himself she was fine, put to rest his loneliness, but he hesitated. Virnie was there, too. He didn't know if he liked the idea or not. Or perhaps he knew the answer and shied away from it.

He rode Noble to the corrals, unsaddled him and took his time about rubbing him down all the while telling himself his only reason for not rushing to the house as he normally would after being away was because of his concern for his horse.

But soon he had no more excuses.

He must face what lay beyond the door across the yard. And what lay within his heart. Things he'd been trying to escape all week. Of course, Gabe's constant yatter about the pretty schoolmarm made it impossible. But even on the ride home, alone with his thoughts, he hadn't been able to escape thinking of Virnie.

Stupid. Stupid. He knew she would be anxious for him to return but only so she could go back to her safe little room at the Maxwells'. No doubt she'd had more than enough of pioneer life by now. He tried to convince himself he didn't care nor expect anything different.

But still he found reason to pause at the corral gate and adjust the bar. He discovered a great need to check the corner post to make sure it was sound. He found an undeniable urge to give a good look around to make sure his fields were still there. He snorted. Like someone could walk away with ten acres. Finally he forced himself to the house, stopping outside the door to gather up his strength to face—what? Disappointment? He had only invited her to stay with Rae. Nothing more. Of course she'd leave as soon as he returned. So what did he need to face then? He sighed and reluctantly acknowledged this house signified a dream that had died with Irene. A dream of home and security and belonging and warmth and—

The dream was dead. Long live reality.

He shoved the door open and staggered back as Rae launched herself into his arms.

"Welcome home, Pa. It's a special occasion. I love you."

He squeezed her tight, and recognizing the game

they had played for years, he said, "I guess if it's a special occasion, I love you, too."

She giggled. "You love me anytime."

He buried his face in her hair. It smelled sweet and clean. Slowly he raised his gaze and his heart punched a hole clear through his reason as Virnie stood before him smiling a welcome. He glanced about the room. It positively shone. The hole in his reason widened. This was how he imagined the house looking when he had lovingly built it. He jerked his gaze to the stove where pots stood waiting. The scent of roast beef and potatoes caused a flood of hunger. He missed good meals. He tried to stop himself from looking back at Virnie but couldn't. His willpower had turned all mushy.

She continued to smile. "Welcome home. We've made supper for you."

He let Rae slip to the floor. She continued to press to his side. He squeezed her shoulder, needing something solid to anchor himself to.

He wanted someone to share his life, his home, his daughter. He wanted someone to welcome him home. Someone who would share responsibility in every way, from preparing tasty meals to cleaning the house to—reality kicked in with a vengeance that froze every other emotion.

What he wanted and needed included a woman able to tackle whatever challenges this fledgling country sent. And Miss Virnie White was not that sort of woman. Too soft and pretty to be truly practical.

He pushed his dreams back into the grave and turned to hang his hat and coat on a hook. Right next to a pretty cape and wide-brimmed hat that surely belonged to Virnie. He inadvertently brushed the cape, lifting the scent of sunshine and flowers to his nostrils. For a moment he couldn't move as his insides responded to the scent. For a heartbeat he let it lift his thoughts from reality. His dreams weren't about to rest in peace nor to allow him peace.

Rae grabbed his hand and tugged him toward the table. "We made a nice meal. A real meal."

"We?" He cocked an eyebrow at Rae but his eyes found their way to Virnie who stood demurely to one side, her hands clasped ladylike at her waist and her smile gentle and cautious, almost impatient. Had she been keeping the meal warm for some time?

"Rachael is a wonderful help," Virnie said.

He turned his attention back to his daughter. "Rae can do most anything she sets her mind to."

Rae rewarded him with a blinding smile. "I'm tough."

"That you are," he agreed.

"The meal is ready." Virnie's voice remained low with no hint of disapproval but Conor would not look her way to see how she'd reacted to Rae's pride in being tough. He didn't want to deal with it. Not tonight. Not with the house clean and a meal on the table. For today, he would accept the gifts without worrying about what the giver thought of him.

He washed up and sat at one end of the table. Virnie sat at the other end and Rae on the side between them. He trailed a finger over the wood, remembering how he had planed and polished it to smooth perfection. Then, realizing what he was doing, he pulled his hands to his lap. The table didn't matter any longer. Any more than the rest of his dreams. Dead. Gone.

"Would you like to say grace?"

Virnie's question pulled him from his mental meanderings. He nodded. Been a long time since he'd felt the need to thank God for anything. He wasn't sure he should be grateful now. No, he was wrong. For the food ready to eat, he was thankful. As to the other stuff—his resurrected dreams, the gentle woman at the end of the table who was responsible for their revival—perhaps that was his own fault. He should have never asked her to stay with Rae.

But he appreciated a good meal and he bowed his head. "Our Father in heaven, hallowed be Your name." He stumbled. He hadn't intended to say the Lord's Prayer. "We're grateful for food and home and blessings. Amen."

"Amen," Virnie whispered. She met his gaze briefly then shied away as she reached for the bowl of little potatoes. "Rachael told me what you liked to eat and we've done our best with what we could find."

His jaw tensed. Did he hear a barely hidden criticism of how little she'd found? "Found your way to the store for meat?"

Virnie blinked, either surprised or defensive. He wasn't sure which. "Rae said it was all right but perhaps I shouldn't have—"

"No. Rae's right. Mr. Brown knows to let her buy supplies if she needs to."

"Good, because she really wanted to make a real meal. Her words."

Conor relaxed and grinned at Rae. "Getting tired of my cooking?"

Rae giggled. "Pa, you don't cook. You open a can."

Conor felt defensive color creeping up his neck and gave Rae a playful cuff to cover his embarrassment. "Never heard you complain before."

"'Cause I was hungry."

He filled his plate with slices of beef, a stack of potatoes, some carrots and drowned it all in rich, brown gravy.

"Rachael prepared the potatoes and carrots," Virnie said.

"Sure are scrawny carrots. Where did you get them?"

Rae answered even though Conor sent a quick

glance at Virnie. "We found them and the 'tatoes in the garden."

Conor blinked and stared at Rae. "I plumb forgot about it." He tasted a carrot then bit into one potato. "Good."

Rae and Virnie exchanged glances. Rae giggled and Virnie ducked her head but not before he caught a look of amusement.

"What's so funny?"

Rae pressed her hand to her mouth to hide her giggles.

Conor silently demanded an answer from Virnie.

She wiped the smile from her lips. "We decided you expect garden plants to be tough, too. No coddling them by pulling weeds." Her eyes danced with amusement.

He had the feeling he was being teased, his tough-routine being gently mocked. But he had no idea how to respond and turned his attention to the food. "Excellent meal," he said when he'd scraped the plate thoroughly. He eyed Rae, wondering when she would be old enough to prepare such meals.

As if reading his thoughts, Virnie spoke. "There are things Rachael could learn to prepare even though she's young. Simple meals that would be more satisfying than eating out of cans. I'd be willing to teach her if you like."

Conor's insides knotted with warring emotions.

He had to let his dreams remain buried and in the hour he'd been back home, he knew having Virnie in the house made that impossible. Seeing her hand in every item in his house, seeing her smiling across the table, feeling her quiet spirit blessing his home were dangerous things to acknowledge to liking but admit them, he did. He should refuse her offer.

On the other hand, he'd like to eat better. Rae needed to eat better, too. And she needed help learning to cook. Help he couldn't provide.

"Would you like that, Rae?"

If she showed the least resistance it might give him the ability to say no to Virnie.

But Rae almost bounced off her chair. "I'd love it, Pa." She looked at Virnie, her eyes shining.

Conor understood it wasn't the idea of learning to cook she liked so much as the thought of Virnie's attention. He had second thoughts. Third thoughts. But none of them quelled the arguing idea of how good this would be for Rae. Not even in the deepest, darkest corners of his heart would he admit it was not for Rae but for himself. "Perhaps we could work something out."

Chapter Five

They agreed on three afternoons a week. Virnie assured herself that would enable her plenty of time to deal with her teaching responsibilities. She would not allow herself to neglect any of the other children and their needs.

The only stipulation Conor had made was, "So long as you don't interfere with my teaching Rae to be tough."

Virnie figured there were ways to show him a woman could handle pioneer life without acting like and dressing like a man and being so tough.

That was her sole reason for going—to teach Conor to accept Rachael as a girl and help prepare the child to cope without a mother.

It had nothing to do with the way her heart skidded sideways whenever Conor walked into the house and glanced at her with a mixture of resistance and—

And what? He had offered her nothing more than tolerance and she wanted nothing more.

She wondered how she could silence the argumentative voice itemizing the reasons to the contrary—his obvious love for Rachael, which he tried unsuccessfully to mask, the beauty of his home that surely revealed deep longings in the man.

Longings dead and buried along with his wife.

But she was helping Rachael as Miss Price had helped her. That's what mattered.

So she concentrated on showing Rachael how to make a pot of vegetable soup.

But Conor did not show up at the usual time.

"He must have found something important to do," Rachael reassured her.

"This happen often?" She had scary visions of Rachael alone after dark. Yes, she understood Rachael must face the realities of her life. And certainly other children stayed alone for short periods of time out of necessity, but this child was not yet nine.

Rachael shrugged. "Sometimes he gets busy."

Virnie wished she could be as unconcerned as Rachael who picked at a slice of bread. But her stomach coiled and recoiled. Conor could take care of himself. He surely didn't need to rush home to see that Rachael was safe. He knew Virnie was with her. But the sense of dread would not leave her.

She stared out the window into the late afternoon

sun. It wouldn't set for a couple of hours yet. And Rachael would not be alone. Virnie would stay until Conor returned.

She tried to stop her thoughts from skipping backward to a time she was about Rachael's age. No, younger because…

She was alone in the dark. Mama was gone. Papa was gone. Miles was gone. She didn't know where they were or when they'd be back. Or were they coming back? Hadn't Papa said, "No. She's not coming back. Never." Or was that Mama?

Mama was gone. She remembered now. And not coming back. Papa kept saying it until he got angry at her.

But where was Papa? Gone, too? And Miles? He'd been the one who held her as she cried because Mama wasn't coming back. He'd promised to look after her. But he was gone, too.

She shivered as she huddled in the corner. Everyone was gone but Virnie.

She couldn't remember how long she'd remained there, crying, certain she'd been abandoned. It had seemed like forever. When the outside door opened, her terror had increased a thousand-fold. They were coming to take her away, too.

A golden glow signaled someone lighting a lamp.

"Virnie, are you here? Where are you?"

It was Miles. He'd come back.

Miles had found her sobbing in the corner, pulled her to his lap and wiped her eyes. "Did you forget I went to work at Mr. Zingle's farm? I told you I would be back after dark."

Papa had come in then. "Too bad she ain't a boy. You could take her with you."

She remembered Miles putting her down and pushing to his feet. "Boy or girl, I'm taking her when she isn't in school."

Papa shrugged. "Might be for the best. I ain't got time to babysit her."

Virnie shuddered at the vivid picture, then pushed it back, back, back into the room of forbidden memories. She needed something to keep her hands and mind busy. "Let's make a bouquet for the table."

"A bouquet?"

"Yes, something pretty—" Remembering the normal Russell objection to pretty, she found a different explanation. "Something to remind us of God's gifts of the season—the harvest, the cooler weather, His provision of things to see us through the winter."

"All right."

Virnie found a pair of shears and a basket to carry their findings. Staying close to the house, watching for Conor's return as she worked, they sought out stalks of grain, a branch with some burnt orange leaves and two bluebells. Virnie's thoughts were unsettled by the flash from her past. But perhaps

God had sent it to make her realize how Rachael might have similar fears. She prayed for a way to discover how the child felt but knew she'd been taught to hide her fears.

They carried their find back to the house and arranged it in a blue granite jug, which they put in the center of the table. Virnie decided it was too tall and distracting. She wouldn't be able to see Conor without tilting to one side or the other. "Let's put it on the sideboard."

Rachael chose the spot. As they stood back to admire their work, they heard a horse riding into the yard.

Rachael raced to the window. "It's Pa. He's back. He always comes back." There seemed to be nothing but confidence and acceptance in her voice.

Perhaps Conor was right. Perhaps teaching Rachael to be strong made it possible to face being alone without fear.

Darkness had fallen by the time the meal was finished. The first time Virnie helped Rachael she had planned to slip back to the Maxwells' before the meal was served but Conor would not allow it.

"Inhospitable." He'd practically growled the word.

Rather than argue, Virnie agreed to share the meals she helped prepare. And it certainly caused her no hardship to do so. She would allow herself to admit she enjoyed playing house in this home. Temporarily, of course.

She insisted on helping with the dishes then reached for her hat and cape. "I best be getting back." She still had some papers to grade and lessons to prepare for the next day.

"We'll walk you back." Conor reached for his hat.

"That's not necessary. It's three miles and then you'll have to turn around and walk back."

Conor handed Rachael a sweater. "It's dark. We'll see you get home safely."

Virnie wanted to argue. This went beyond helping Rachael. It slipped past barriers, her rationalizations and headed straight for a tender spot in her heart where someone actually cared about her safety and security. It was a dangerous place to visit and certainly not a need she wanted to set free. "Conor, really, I don't need an escort. I'm used to being on my own."

He stepped outside and waited. "It's my fault for being late."

Rachael, set to dash down the road, paused to announce, "Virnie was worried about you."

Conor blinked in astonishment. "Miss White," he corrected Rachael but she had already run along the path, waving her arms and singing. He turned to stare at Virnie. "You were worried?"

"It's just that I remember what it was like to be alone after dark." She marched after Rachael.

Conor didn't move. "Rae isn't afraid of the dark. Are you?"

She couldn't explain how it felt to be alone and uncertain if anyone cared. "Not of the dark."

He caught up to her. She felt his measured study and was grateful for the dusk to hide her expression. He saw only her weakness. Not unlike her father who found her weak and useless. Only she wasn't. Not anymore.

"Rae loves the dark. Look at her." Conor sounded pleased by the way Rachael ran ahead, almost disappearing into the gloom. "She can face almost any challenge."

"You have every right to be proud of her." She half expected him to deny it.

"I guess I do. She's proving to be a good pioneer girl. Together we'll build us a solid future."

He was not like her father, she again discovered. He adored his daughter and sought only to prepare her to deal with the life he had chosen for them. She might not agree with all his methods but she couldn't deny his affection.

Ahead of them, Rachael stopped and tiptoed toward the edge of the field alongside the road. She squatted down.

"She's found something." Conor picked up his pace. "What is it?"

"Pa, it's a baby kitten."

Virnie and Conor reached Rachael at the same time. She held a tiny mite of a cat, too young to be on its own and squalling frantically.

"It's crying for its mama. Poor little kitty." Rachael cuddled it against her neck and giggled when the kitten nuzzled about searching about for something to eat. "She's hungry."

"It's too small to be of any use. Give it to me and I'll take care of it." But when Conor reached for the kitten, Rachael backed away.

"I want to keep it."

"Rae, it's just a useless little kitten. I doubt it will even survive."

"No. I'll feed it and take care of it. It will live. You'll see. It will be a good cat."

Conor sighed. "What good is a scrawny little thing like that?"

Until now Virnie had been content to stand back and watch, but hearing the harsh condemnation in Conor's voice seared her insides. Just because something was small and defenseless didn't make it valueless.

Rachael appealed to her. "Miss White, don't you think I should keep this kitten?"

She stilled her arguments. This wasn't about her. It was only about a helpless kitten. "A cat is good for keeping the mice down."

"This scrawny thing?" Conor's voice rang with scorn.

She faced him and smiled. Even in the dusk she could see him hesitate, caught between his need to always be practical and the longing in Rachael's voice. "You might be surprised what this scrawny cat will grow into."

He stared into her eyes but it was thankfully too dark for her to be able to guess what he thought of her remark. She could only hope he didn't read anything more than a vote to give the kitten a chance. She didn't want him wondering if her remark held far more personal information.

He nodded. "Very well. You can see if you can keep the thing alive. But no moaning and crying when it dies."

"It won't," Rachael protested hotly. "And I wouldn't cry. You know I wouldn't."

"We'll see."

"You want to hold her, Miss White?" Rachael held out the kitten for Virnie to take.

She cupped it in her palms. "It's soft. And such a pretty color. All gray." She examined it more closely. "With little white tips on all four paws."

"I'm going to call it Tippy."

Conor groaned. "You name it and it will only hurt more when it dies."

"Tippy isn't going to die." Rachael took the kitten

back and held it close as if protecting it from Conor's dire prediction. She hurried ahead.

Conor groaned again.

Virnie stifled a giggle at his frustration.

He heard her. "Don't laugh." They continued their journey toward Sterling. "But I suppose she might as well learn the cycle of life and death in this country."

"I expect she's plenty familiar with it. After all, her mother died." She couldn't keep the memory of her own loss from edging her words.

Conor didn't speak for a moment. "I guess you have a point though I don't know how much she remembers. Or if she thinks about it ever."

"She does."

They walked on in silence for a few steps.

"She's said things to you?"

Virnie couldn't reveal Rachael's secret but Conor ought to know that Rachael hadn't forgotten. "Just enough for me to know she remembers her mother but is afraid of forgetting her."

He stopped, forcing her to stop, too, or walk away from him. She was too curious about his reaction to walk away. "I want her to forget. She can't hold on to the past."

"Conor, she can't forget. And if she does it will cause her more pain and distress than remembering."

"How can you say that? Is it a theory they teach

all fledgling teachers?" His voice rasped and she guessed his concern for his daughter caused it. Or perhaps he was dealing with his own pain and distress at remembering.

"They don't tell teachers that. I speak from personal experience. My mother died when I was five. I can't remember anything about her. Not what she looked like. Not the sound of her voice. Not her scent. I can't even remember her holding me." She realized her voice grew thin as if her the tension of her innards held her throat captive.

Conor lightly clasped her elbow. "I'm sorry." He pulled his hand away.

The touch was brief, quick, as if he thought better of his action as soon as he made it, but brief as it was, it touched far more than her skin. It melted her tension and filled her with a strange mixture of regret and longing, of loneliness and hope. She scrubbed her lips together as she fought for a solid core of purpose as she had taught herself to do. But she couldn't find it and jerked around, making her feet move down the road, trailing after Rachael.

Conor easily kept pace with her. "I always thought it was best to erase any memory of Irene. That's Rae's mother."

She noticed he said Rae's mother and not his wife, and wondered if he tried to erase Irene's memory from his own thoughts. She wanted to explain the futility of insisting on forgetfulness. "I've tried to forget things in my past but it seems I remember the things I don't want to remember and forget the ones I wish I could remember."

"What do you try and forget?"

Her heart cried out to tell him, perhaps receive another gentle touch of sympathy, but for too long she'd pushed those things into hiding and she feared bringing them out. "Just stuff. I expect we all have things we don't want to remember."

He sighed. "You're right there."

She ached to ask him about the things he wanted to forget, perhaps offer a bit of sympathy in return but her emotions frightened her. The intensity of her longing for something beyond being a teacher, her desire to reach out to Conor—they were all too unfamiliar and taking her away from the safe boundaries she had created for her life. And so they walked on in silence, hearing only Rachael's murmuring to her new pet and the soft sounds of the evening—a night bird cooing, the grass rustling in the breeze and, as they neared town, the warning bark of someone's dog.

Sunday morning, Rae turned to Conor. "Pa, I'd sure like to go to church."

Conor laughed. "Last time I checked Christmas was months away." He made a habit of attending regularly—Christmas and Easter. Saw no need of more. Attending every Sunday sure hadn't helped Irene cope with life.

"I know but I went with Virnie and liked it. Besides, I could see Alice Morgan. She's my best friend."

Conor shrugged. He didn't suppose going more often would turn either of them into sissies. "Sure. I got nothing better to do."

Rae ran to her bedroom. She emerged a few minutes later in a dress. A dress! "Where'd you get that?"

"Grandma Russell sent for Christmas, 'member?"

He surely didn't. Then he noticed how she'd attempted to braid her hair and tie it with ribbons matching her dress. He wouldn't ask if Grandma had sent those, too. He didn't want to know.

He knew two days ago when he saw the jug on the sideboard full of flowery stuff that he'd made a mistake.

He was certain of it when Virnie convinced him to let Rae keep the kitten who had refused to die.

His certainty grew when he felt an incredible urge to comfort her when she made her painful confession about not being able to remember her mother.

But seeing Rae in a dress, her hair fussed with, proved it beyond a shadow.

He had to put a stop to Virnie hanging about.

"Why did you get all dolled up?"

Rae shot him a look faintly reminiscent of Virnie's disbelieving looks. "You'd put on your best clothes for the president, wouldn't you?"

"That sounds like something Virnie would say."

"It's true, isn't it?"

He couldn't argue with her self-assured logic. "Just don't think it will get you out of your chores."

"I ever miss a day yet?"

"Come on, let's go. You sure you can ride in a skirt?"

"I 'spect I can if I want."

Shaking his head, he swung to Noble's back and pulled Rae up beside him. Yup. She managed just fine in a skirt. And why that should annoy him half to death made no sense.

When they arrived at the church, he dropped her to her feet. She waited as he hitched Noble then took his hand as they walked inside. He glanced upward but the rafters didn't threaten to collapse at his unscheduled visit.

He followed Rae into a pew, realizing too late that she chose to sit next to Virnie. So much for putting her from his mind.

She smiled at him then turned her attention to Rae.

He stared at the top of Virnie's head. Or rather the top of her bonnet. A very pretty bonnet but of absolutely no use whatsoever. She wore a nice dress, gray as a soft evening with little frills around the collar. Practical enough for a teacher but a pioneer? Why he could just imagine how she would fuss if she had to get it dirty. No, sir. She wasn't made for pioneering. He resisted an urge to slap his forehead. Who was asking her to be a pioneer? Certainly not him.

At that point she lifted her head and met his look. Her brown eyes filled with what he could only take as appreciation. For what? Bringing Rae to church? But her soft brown gaze wrung out all his firm reasons and hung them to dry. No, she wasn't hardy enough for pioneering but he wished she were. He wished he could dream of sharing his life with her, having her help him build a future together.

The pastor called them to worship and Conor gladly turned his attention to the front.

He would tell her right after church that they had no more need for her to come to the farm.

But the sermon had been about God's sufficiency and had filled Conor with a queer mix of doubt and hope. He wanted to think God could meet all his needs but he feared opening his hands and releasing self-control. He was so muddled by his thoughts that he plumb forgot his intention to tell Virnie not to come anymore. It didn't escape his attention that he found the excuse very convenient.

And Monday when Virnie came to the farm and

made a very nice meal of fried chicken and biscuits, making sure to report how Rae had helped, well, it seemed downright unnecessary to forgo the good meals and the cooking lessons for Rae.

She came twice more that week and twice more there were downright good reasons not to ask her to stop coming. Real good solid reasons that had absolutely nothing to do with the fact he counted the hours until she showed up, practically writhing with disappointment the days she didn't come. No, sir. It had nothing to do with that.

Since the Sunday when Conor had dropped to the pew beside her, since their gazes had connected and she'd felt a deep sense of welcome—which she knew made no sense—Virnie had to restrain herself from going to the farm every day. So far, she had excused her visits as helping Rachael and answered the few questions from the townspeople about her trips as helping Rachael learn to cope on her own.

Only she didn't believe it anymore.

She continued to go because the days she didn't felt empty in a way she'd never experienced before. She found herself storing up little stories to tell Conor about the games the children had played at school or the way she'd been able to help the Schmidt boys or how Hilda Morgan had written such a lovely poem.

And she loved hearing about his day. The work

he'd done, his plans for the winter and for next year's crop and the little things he'd thought noteworthy.

She knew something had shifted between them but she couldn't say how or why it mattered. Perhaps it was only a truce—a silent agreement to overlook their differences and enjoy the present without regard to the future or past. The past she had no trouble dismissing but the future was a different matter. One she didn't want to deal with. She had her future clearly mapped out—imitate Miss Price in being a teacher who dedicated her entire life to helping children.

The fact that the idea no longer filled her with intense longing and pride didn't matter. It was what she wanted to do.

Today was bright and sunny. Too nice to be indoors enduring the heat of the cook stove.

She turned to Rachael. "Let's go to the garden and see how many carrots and potatoes we can find. They need to be dug before the frost comes."

Rachael didn't have to be asked twice. She threw down the dusting rag and abandoned the task Virnie had assigned her of dusting all the furniture.

Virnie had found it necessary to whack great huge weeds out of her way for the few potatoes she'd already uncovered. She whacked more out of the way now and swung the spade to clear a path down what she guessed to be the row of potatoes. A great cloud of dust and weed seeds billowed up and she coughed and turned away. Her shift in direction allowed her to stare across the field to where Conor plowed down the stubble. For the most part he walked in dust from his task. The ground needed a rain. Or snow. But Conor wanted to finish the plowing first. She knew he worked from dawn to dusk trying to accomplish the task.

He reached the end of the field and turned the horse for the return trip. He paused to wipe his face with a big blue hanky. He stared her direction. It was too far to know if he saw her but then he waved. Just a quick little salute as if he'd acknowledged her unintentionally.

She lifted her hand in response. As she lowered her hand, she curled her fingers as if she could grasp and hold forever the way her heart rejoiced at his wave. It was nothing. He would have waved to any passing neighbor. Only she wasn't a neighbor. He didn't have to look her direction. He didn't have to acknowledge her at all.

But he had.

Smiling, she turned back to the garden calling Rachael from playing with the kitten to help as she dug potatoes. "You put them in the gunnysack."

Several times, she took a break from searching for the root vegetables and straightened. But each time she managed to catch Conor with his back to them. Not that she expected him to wave again. That was plumb silly. Yet a vast emptiness sucked at her lungs each time. It felt suspiciously like disappointment but she denied it hotly.

The sun began its descent toward the western horizon by the time Rachael and Virnie stood at the edge of the garden, now a tangled mess of bent weeds and freshly dug soil.

"Three bags of vegetables," Rachael announced.

"Not bad for a neglected garden."

She glanced toward the field. Conor was on the last furrow. He would soon be in for supper. The thought brought such a pleasant taste of honey to her thoughts that she lifted her face to the sun and smiled.

Rachael chased her kitten through the weeds, laughing as they played a game of hide-and-seek.

The harnesses jingled and Conor called to the horse as he walked the plough across the yard and unhitched the horse.

Virnie knew he would rub the animal down and see it had water and feed before he tended to his own needs, which, she grinned as she saw his dirty face, included a good wash. He had rolled his sleeves to the elbows, revealing muscular arms darkened by the sun. Broad shoulders filled out his faded blue shirt. His dark trousers were liberally coated with dust. A battered hat protected his head but the exposed hair had turned from black to brown from the good earth that settled there after he'd stirred it up.

He met her eyes over the yard and smiled, his teeth flashing white in his dust-covered face.

She nodded and smiled. There was something very appealing about a working man.

She jerked her thoughts back to reality. For a moment she watched Rachael play. How she enjoyed being part of all this. Helping Rachael, making meals, keeping the house clean and tidy and waiting for Conor to come home for supper, even rescuing the meager garden produce. This was only temporary, a pretend life that couldn't be hers. She and Conor—

Enough silly mental games. She took off the gloves she had borrowed from the house and tossed them on top of the shovel. She shook the dust from her skirt and wiped her face with a hanky.

"Do you have someplace to store them?"

Rachael returned carrying little Tippy. "We have a root cellar. Sometimes I like to play there when it's hot outside. It's always nice and cool in there."

"Of course." She'd seen the hump behind the hill and the three steps descending to a narrow door. "I suppose these vegetables will keep better there. Help me drag them over." The bags weighed more than she could carry. But with Rachael pushing and her pulling, they managed to get them to the steps to the root cellar. Getting them down the steps would be no problem. If she had the door open, perhaps the momentum would allow her to get them inside.

"Wait here while I open the door then we'll push the bags down."

Rachael sat on the top step, more interested in Tippy than the potatoes and carrots. Virnie knew in the middle of winter the Russells would be grateful for her foresight in making sure they had them.

The door stuck at one corner. She pushed at it with her shoulder. It slowly creaked back. She didn't move—not one muscle as she stared at cobwebs hanging from the corner of the doorway and clinging to the top of the door, waving and quivering.

Her skin crawled like it was alive with spiders. She shuddered. Her teeth chattered. Her heart grabbed her throat and squeezed off her air. One long, dusty mat of webs swung free of the door toward her.

She screamed as terror erased every thought but escape. She dashed up the steps, panting as if she had run all the way from town. Frantically, she brushed her hair, her arms and shook her skirts. "Ugh," she groaned.

"The pretty little teacher is afraid of getting dirty." Conor stood beside the bags, his fists balled on his hips. He laughed. A very unpleasant mocking sound that scraped along Virnie's nerves. However, it failed to erase the crawly feeling of spiders.

She shuddered. "I hate spiders." The look she gave him dared him to laugh at that.

He didn't laugh but his wide grin was just as bad.

She felt an incredible urge to stomp on something. Like every spider within a hundred-mile radius. Or even better, a smiling, mocking man who would no doubt take her fear of spiders and turn it into a full-length serial about the weakness of women in general and schoolteachers in particular. "Put your own stupid vegetables in the root cellar. Or leave them to freeze. I don't care." She spun on her heel and marched for the house.

"Pa, I think you made her mad."

Conor chuckled. "'Pears maybe I did."

Virnie didn't slow down until she was safe inside the house. The man would do well to choose more wisely his times to be amused at her expense.

Chapter Six

Conor didn't know what possessed him to say what he did to Virnie. He'd enjoyed watching her dig in the garden. Resented the time it took to go north the length of the field knowing she was within sight but he had to keep his back to her. And the south length seemed to go far too quickly as he watched her in the garden.

She'd whacked at the weeds, jabbed the spade into the soil and crouched on the ground, digging for the hidden little nuggets of vegetables.

He'd been too far away to be able to see her face clearly but he saw the dust rising from her work and suspected she would be getting down and out dirty. And he grinned. Virnie White grubbing in the soil, getting soiled. The idea warmed the bottom of his heart. Melted away resistance.

It wasn't until he put away the harness and tended

the horse that he realized how foolish his thoughts had grown.

Virnie didn't belong on a farm. He knew only a tough, hard, strong woman could survive this sort of life. Digging in the garden was child's play compared to some of the tasks she would face. Raging storms, wild animals, sickness with no medical help available. This was not a life for a pretty little thing like Virnie.

By the time he left the barn, his resentment at her had reached unreasonable proportions.

And his insides felt as if he'd walked through snowstorm breathing in sharp, razor-like frozen pellets.

Seeing Virnie run screaming from the root cellar had solidified his rationale. She did not belong on the farm. His laugh had been as much at himself as at her. Not that she knew it. Nor would he tell her. But he had let himself veer far from the reality of his life.

This was a good reminder to pull his thoughts back where they belonged—on survival.

He took his time putting the sacks in the cellar, grunting under their weight. "How did Miss White get these bags here?"

"I helped her." Rae obviously thought that enough explanation.

He closed the door tightly and stared at the house

wondering if he should stay away until Virnie left. "Do you suppose supper is ready?"

"It's stew so it's ready."

Stew. His mouth flooded with anticipation. He loved stew. He'd worked hard all day and he was hungry. Still he hesitated.

Rae squinted up at him. "You scared because Miss White is mad at you?"

"Scared? Nah. Not me." But he was nervous. Would she find a way to punish him? Or—

Would she refuse to come again?

He scowled into the bright sky. Good thing if she did. It was what he wanted. Wasn't it? So why did his mind suddenly scramble for ways to apologize and convince her it was only harmless amusement?

Rae pulled at his hand. "Come on, Pa. I'm hungry."

He allowed her to tug him toward the house, his insides warring unmercifully over his conflicting reactions. He'd been trying to find a way to tell her not to come. But not like this. Not with unresolved anger between them.

He let out a whoosh of air as relief stilled his confused emotions. That's all it was. Concern about the anger. He'd do his best to resolve that. *Then* he'd figure out a nice way of telling her not to come again. "Wait." He glanced around, then saw several stalks of golden wheat at the edge of the field. He jogged over and cut them clean.

"What's that for?" Rae demanded.

"Thought Virnie might like them for the jug of flowery things she keeps on the sideboard."

Rae stared. "Thought you said they were useless pretty things."

"I might have."

Rae slowly grinned. "You want Miss White to like you." She started to giggle

He snorted. "I just don't want her to be mad at me."

Rae giggled the rest of the way to the house.

Conor put his hands on her shoulders at the doorway. "Now you be quiet. I don't want her wondering if I'm still laughing at her or if you are. That's what made her angry in the first place."

Rae sobered. "I wouldn't laugh at her."

"Fine." He pushed the door open.

Virnie stood at the stove, her back to him, the stiffening of her shoulder the only sign she heard him step into the room.

He stood with a handful of wheat stalks, feeling about as foolish and awkward as a seventeen-year-old meeting his future father-in-law. "Brought you something."

She took her time about setting a spoon down and turning. "Yes?"

He held out the wheat. "Thought this might look nice in the jug." He tipped his chin toward the sideboard.

Confusion and surprise chased across her face as she took the stalks. "Thank you." Then she faced him squarely, her eyes fierce with some kind of challenge. "It's just a useless bunch of pretty things."

He nodded. "Guess it ain't hurting anything." He wasn't sure what he meant. Perhaps that there was a time and place for pretty. Just as there was a time and place for tough and hard. Trouble was the latter belonged on a frontier farm. And pretty belonged in a house, sheltered and protected. A long aching loneliness, a sad wish it could be different, made his chest feel like a giant weight had settled there.

"Thank you." She placed the stalks in the jug, rearranging them to her liking. She turned to see he had remained rooted to the spot watching, wanting and fully aware how useless such feelings were.

"I didn't mean to laugh at you."

She grinned. "I expect it was funny to see me run screaming from such harmless things." Her smile flattened and her eyes grew wide, stark. "I hate spiders. Ugh."

"Uh-huh." Now if he could eliminate spiders from the world… Well, it was as impossible as thinking she might fit into his life.

"Supper is ready." She waved toward the table.

"Let me wash up."

The next day Virnie paused from dusting the furniture to study the jug with the stalks of wheat.

It meant nothing. Just some unharvested wheat he'd given her by way of apology.

Only it meant so much more. He'd allowed there was a place for pretty things that served no purpose except to make the house more pleasant.

But it meant even more to her foolish, errant heart. It meant he cared that it mattered to her. She ducked her head and closed her eyes. Why were her thoughts being so disobedient?

She turned away and went to the table where she was showing Rachael how to make a meatloaf. She didn't expect Rachael would remember all her cooking lessons. In fact, she didn't care if she did. For now it was enough to work with the child and see her learning how to cope. And if Conor smiled his appreciation and thanked her after each meal, well, that was nice, too.

Conor dashed into the house. "Rae, I need some help. The bull has a bad cut on his leg that needs doctoring but I can't get him in by myself."

Virnie could hear the bull raging with pain and frustration outside. She glanced out the window as Rachael ran after her father. The pair of them struggled to get the bull headed for the barn. Virnie gasped as the bull lowered his head and charged toward Rachael. She'd be hurt. She dropped the tea towel she held and ran to help them. They had managed to get the bull in the barn and she hurried to the interior.

Conor danced back and forth, waving his arms and trying to direct the bull toward a pen. Rachael stood at the rails with a long pole ready to slide it in behind the bull and stop him from backing out once he was persuaded to step into the pen.

Conor prodded the bull into place. "Rae, the pole."

She pushed it across but the bull backed up, caught the pole partway and tossed Rachael to the ground. Conor rescued the pole and jammed it into place, trapping the bull. The animal couldn't back up but he could paw at the boards in front of him and toss his head.

Virnie saw what the bull needed. She grabbed a rope. "Let me help."

Conor snickered. "You going to lecture him or sweet-talk him?"

She sent him a look fit to make him repentant. "You might be surprised by the effectiveness of a little sweet talk." And to prove her point she murmured softly to the bull as she gathered her skirts and climbed the bars of the fence, reaching toward the bull's head.

"Hang on, you'll get hurt," Conor warned. "Step back."

She ignored his order. "I know what I'm doing." She waited for the bull to lower his head, snagged the rope around his ears and in quick movements fashioned a neat halter and snubbed the rope to the fence. The bull jerked back but he was effectively restrained. She climbed down, shook out her skirts and patted her hands. "There you go. Do your thing on that wound."

Conor's hands hung at his sides as he stared openmouthed.

Rachael climbed out from the adjoining pen and stared as well.

Virnie grinned. She took great delight in surprising them both. "Shows you what a little schoolmarm is capable of."

Conor seemed too stunned to move.

"Don't you have something you need to do?" She waved toward the animal.

He gathered up his vet supplies, all the while darting wide-eyed glances her direction.

"Do you need me to stay and help?" She managed to sound innocent though she suspected her eyes gave her away. She could feel them dancing with amusement.

"Uh. No. I can manage." He went to the side of the pen and reached through the boards to tend to the wound.

"Well. Then I'll leave you to it." She managed to contain herself until she reached the house where she leaned against the door and laughed loud and hard.

She hummed as she finished meal preparations. Rachael had remained with Conor but she didn't mind. She enjoyed the time to herself, allowing a chuckle now and then in private without anyone to ask what was so funny.

The two of them returned.

"Did you get him fixed up?" Her question was reasonable enough even if the way her words rounded with amusement made Conor shoot her a bewildered look.

"Pa cleaned the cut good and said the old boy would be like new in a few days."

"That's good."

They sat around the table. Conor said grace. They passed the food. Nothing new. They'd done it numerous times. But something had changed. She felt it in the air between them, in the look he gave her and in the bubbling excitement in her heart.

Conor ducked outside as soon as he finished eating. She smiled at his departing figure. She had set him back on his heels and she understood he didn't like it.

She and Rachael cleaned the kitchen. Still Conor did not return. She wondered if she should leave until he did. "You better start your homework," she told Rachael. She wandered over to stare out the window. "I'm going to see if your pa is in the barn."

Rachael had the kitten on her lap and spent more time letting it chase a string she draped over the table edge than she did doing homework. She barely noticed Virnie's announcement.

Virnie slipped out and crossed to the low sod-roofed barn and stepped into the gloom. "Conor, are you here?"

"Right beside you."

She jumped as his low voice came from her right. He stood to the side of a small square window. He would have been able to watch her cross the yard. She quickly ran a hand over her hair. Was everything in place?

"Where did you learn to do that?"

"What? Tidy my hair?"

"No. Halter a bull. Not many women can do that. Lots of men can't, in fact."

She chuckled. "Surprised you, didn't I?"

He laughed, too. "You could say that."

"I have to admit it feels good to surprise Conor Russell."

"Why is that?" He moved closer. In the light from the open door she saw his eyes were dark and watchful.

She met his look without revealing any sign of how her nerves jittered at having him so close. "Because you have it all figured out. Women are weak and useless. There is no place for them on the farm or in your life. And pretty things have no value."

He didn't speak or indicate how her statement affected him.

"Maybe I proved you wrong."

He jerked away. "I don't think you proved anything. I've seen the folly of putting pretty ahead of reality. Of expecting any but the strongest and sturdiest of women to live out here."

Disappointment seared through her. She had hoped he'd admit he was wrong. "You're talking about your wife, aren't you? Hardly seems fair to judge every woman you see by what she did."

He faced her, his face wracked with fury and pain. "What do you know about her? What she did?"

She backed away a step. "All I know is what I see. How you treat Rachael. And what she says about not allowing weakness."

"She's right. There is no room out here for weakness."

"Nice things, pretty things don't signify weakness." She thought of the bouquet on the sideboard and his contribution.

"Yeah, what purpose do they serve?"

"To brighten the days. Seems to me a person can face most anything if their heart is happy. Pretty things do a lot toward that."

His expression hardened. His eyes darkened. "Where did you learn to snub an animal?"

She didn't want to tell him about that part of her

life. Not because Miss Price had told her she was now a lady and she should forget her former life but because she didn't want to confront the pain her past carried.

But Conor moved closer. He touched her shoulder. "What are you hiding?"

The weight of his hand on her shoulder, the soft tone of his voice made her want to tell him everything. Not just how she'd learned to fashion a quick rope halter, but how abandoned she'd felt, how alone and afraid.

She lowered her eyes as she spoke. "I used to follow my brother, Miles, around when he worked on a farm. He said I might as well learn to be useful as be underfoot. He was the one who taught me."

Conor caught her chin and tipped her face up. "What else did he teach you?"

She couldn't move. Couldn't think. Couldn't speak. His gentle touch erased all reason from her mind. She couldn't shift her thoughts from the way his finger ignited such intense longings in her. She had ached most of her life for touches that conveyed such caring and kindness.

"Who taught you to be a prim and proper schoolmarm? Not your brother, I think."

She jerked back and pulled herself to reason. "That would be Miss Price. She raised me from the time I was ten."

"What happened to your brother? I know your mother died but where was your father?"

His question roared through her dragging in its wake all her unwanted memories, scouring her insides with them. She didn't dare let even one of them find words. If she did, how would she ever stop the flow? "It doesn't matter." With limbs as wooden as the door beside her, she jerked around. "I must go now."

She wouldn't go back. Her errant emotions made it too risky. So she set her heart to being the best teacher ever. She made flash cards to spur the Schmidt boys into learning more English words. She searched her texts for problems to challenge George. She began to plan a Christmas program that would involve each child and showcase their strengths. And she wrote a long letter to Miss Price carefully avoiding mention of her tangled emotions regarding Conor. She settled for reporting the progress Rachael had made in learning basic skills.

She managed to stay away from the farm for four days. It was Rachael's hurt expression when she gave excuses that changed her mind.

"I'll go home with you today, Rachael, and see how you have been managing without me." She smiled to prove to herself it was the main reason.

"I washed all the dirty dishes. And put my stuff away."

"Good girl. Help me tidy the schoolroom and then we can go."

Rachael grabbed the broom and did a reasonable job of sweeping. Virnie would give the room another once over before school opened in the morning.

Rachael ran ahead on the way home, leaving Virnie plenty of time to think.

But she knew she returned to the farm for more than Rachael's sake. It was because of Conor. Though she realized how foolish it was to dream he'd see her in a new light—see that she wasn't weak, helpless, useless. She knew why it mattered so much what he thought. Somehow, gaining his approval convinced her she could erase the hurt of her past.

Rachael paused to watch a bug scurry across the road then fell in beside Virnie. "I thought you might be too mad at Pa to come again."

Virnie prayed for wisdom to say the right thing. "I'm sorry you thought that because it isn't true. Your pa and I aren't angry at each other."

"Good. I don't what you to stop coming."

Virnie felt a familiar ache from her childhood. The feeling of abandonment. She couldn't think of any kind way to respond to Rachael's statement. Yet at some point they would both have to face facts. There would be no reason to continue her visits. They would move on in different directions.

She pretended a great interest in the puffy clouds

along the horizon as she struggled with a fresh wave of pain that had nothing to do with her past. She loved Rachael more than a teacher should love one particular student. She wished she could be part of the child's life for more than a few months.

"Pa's been working on the barn."

Thankful for the change in conversation, Virnie asked, "What's he doing?"

"Says it's time to put a proper roof on. Says the sod was only temporary. He's going to put up big—" She put her fingers together in a V to indicate.

"Rafters?"

"Yes. Going to make room for a loft."

"Sounds like an ambitious plan."

"Virnie, what's a loft?"

Rachael had slipped into the habit of using Virnie's given name when they were alone. Virnie enjoyed the sense of closeness it gave her so she never corrected the child. "A loft?" She explained the large attic area for storing hay. "It's fun to play in a loft. When the hay is gone, you can skate on the floor. My brother showed me how."

"You have a brother?"

"Yes, Miles." For a time he had been both mother and father to her. How could she still miss him after all these years?

"Where is he?"

"I'm not sure. I haven't seen him in a very long time."

"I wish I had a brother or sister." She slowed as they neared the Faulk place, watching for any sign of the dog.

"I thought you told me Devin Faulk was gone along with his dog."

"Shh." She held her finger to her lips. "You never know." Her whisper was barely audible.

Just then a snarling black ball of fur erupted from under the porch and barreled toward them.

Virnie's heart landed in her mouth with a shuddering thud. She faced the animal, afraid to take her eyes off the menace.

Rachael whimpered and took one running step before Virnie grabbed her and shoved her behind her back. "Don't run. He'll only chase you." She edged down the road. Where was Mrs. Faulk with her broom? She should have brought her own broom from the school. She glanced to the right and left but apart from some dried blades of grass there was nothing that would serve as a weapon. "Stop," she ordered.

That had about as much effect as a waving a hanky.

"Stop," she shouted. "Tictoc, stop right now."

The animal didn't even slow down.

A door banged. Mrs. Faulk stepped to the porch with her broom.

Thank You, God.

"Tictoc, get back here." Whack.

The dog's snarl ended on a whine.

"Now." A series of whacks. "Don't make me come after you." More whacks.

Tictoc stopped. He turned, made three steps, then spun back to Virnie and Rachael, growling and snarling.

"Tictoc. Now."

Virnie didn't wait to see if the dog would obey. She sidled along the road as fast as she could without running, Rachael clinging to her back.

Not until they were safely away from the threat did Virnie stop and bend over her knees to suck in air. "I see Devin is back."

Rachael scowled in the direction of the Faulk house. "I wish he would go away forever."

Virnie straightened. "Did you ever tell your pa about the dog?"

"I can't."

The danger of this child dealing with the dog on her own made Virnie's knees go weak. "You must. What if Mrs. Faulk isn't there some day? I need you to promise me you'll tell him today."

"He'll think I'm weak. He says the dog is all bluff."

"I don't want to see if that's true or not." She squatted to meet Rachael's eyes full-on. She grabbed the child's shoulders. "This is something you *should* be afraid of. I'm sure your pa will agree."

Rachael didn't look convinced.

Virnie couldn't contemplate what the dog could do to Rachael. "I don't want to see you hurt. Promise me you'll tell your pa. I'll help you if you want."

She could tell Rachael struggled between her fear and her desire to please her father. Virnie waited. Finally Rachael nodded. "You'll stay with me when I tell him?"

"Of course." She hugged the child, relieved this danger would be dealt with.

At the farm she found the floor needed mopping and the stove polishing but Rachael had indeed washed the dishes and the table had been cleared. Virnie stared at the jug on the sideboard. She had expected Conor would have tossed out the pretty things. Instead, she saw several of the old branches of colored leaves had been removed and fresh ones inserted.

Her smile tugged the corners of her heart. Conor had changed. She could almost hope—

She closed her eyes and prayed for strength to be what she knew she must be and ignore the tremors on her heart that made it difficult to think.

Rachael helped her prepare a simple meal of fried eggs and potatoes.

When Conor stepped into the house, Virnie's heart tremors escalated to earthquake proportions. She grabbed her emotions and forced them to submission before she turned to face him.

Sweat soaked his shirt. Dust hid in each fold and

wrinkle. He took off his hat to reveal a dusty rim of hair that had been exposed. "Hello."

The uncertain, husky quality of his voice echoed in her head.

She managed a squeaky, "Hello." She tried to tear her gaze from his but her eyes would not obey. The scent of masculine sweat and dust made her think of hot summer days. Made her wish and want for things she knew did not fit into her well-laid plans.

"Smells good in here." He turned to hang his hat, freeing her from her tangled thoughts.

A mat of cobweb hung from his hair, draping down his back. She shuddered and pointed.

Rachael giggled. "Pa, you're wearing a cob-web."

Conor twisted to look over his back, making the web move like it was alive.

Virnie clamped her fist to her mouth to stop a moan.

"Brush it off," Conor said to Rachael.

Virnie managed to squeeze out one word. "Outside."

Conor glanced at Rachael and they both laughed at her fear but thankfully stepped out the door to brush his back.

"The spiders really like the space under the sods," Conor said as he washed. He made a great pretense of brushing his hair as if seeking for lost spiders. He grinned wickedly at Virnie when she shuddered.

"It's not funny," she muttered.

Conor wisely ducked his head but she knew he found it amusing. But it provided her the perfect opportunity.

"Some fears are good. They prepare us to face danger." She nodded toward Rachael who looked about as eager to talk to Conor as she would be to face Tictoc.

"Rachael, tell him."

Conor's head came up and he alternately studied the two of them. "What's up?"

Rachael ducked her head.

"She has something she needs to tell you," Virnie prompted.

"Rae?"

Slowly, Rachael faced Conor. "Pa, it's Faulks' dog."

"That noisy beast. What about him?"

Rachael sought support from Virnie. She smiled and nodded. "Pa, I'm scared of him."

Conor stared at his daughter then jerked his gaze toward Virnie. "Is this your idea?"

Anger roared up her throat and scalded her tongue. "Rachael, why don't you take some food out to Tippy and play with her for a few minutes."

Rachael looked about to argue but with both Conor and Virnie looking ready to fight, she sighed and dragged herself out the door, pausing once. "I told you I didn't want to tell him."

Virnie waited until the door closed but before she could speak, Conor leaned forward, his forearms on the table, his fists bunched. "I don't want her taught to be afraid of things."

"No one taught her to fear that dog coming after her. If Mrs. Faulk didn't call it off…"

"The dog is all bluff. The worst thing she can do is show fear."

They glowered at each other. What had given her the stupid idea he might have softened? She'd gladly let it go and leave for home, perhaps to never return. She denied the aching protest the idea brought. But for Rachael's safety she must pursue the subject.

"Everyone is afraid of something. Sometimes little and unreasonable things like my fear of spiders. Other things are real and valid. Like Rachael being afraid of that dog. Even you have fears though you'd never admit it."

His scowl deepened. "What am I afraid of?"

"Weakness. You're afraid to allow any weakness will destroy you. You're afraid any softness makes a person vulnerable and useless." She breathed hard. The feeling of being little and useless billowed up inside her with a bitter bile taste. Her father had treated her that way and now Conor had effectively made her feel the same.

She pushed to her feet. "I have to go. I'm sure

you can figure out how to clean the kitchen on your own. Or does doing so indicate weakness?"

Not waiting for his answer, she stomped out. She calmed her anger enough to tiptoe past the Faulk place. Thankfully the dog did not come out though she thought she heard him bark from inside the barn. They ought to be made to keep that animal locked in the barn all the time.

By the time she reached the Maxwells' she'd pushed her anger to the back burner. She was not a weak, useless creature anymore. She was a teacher with the futures of seventeen children to shape and guide. It was what she wanted. All she wanted. She had to remember that.

Chapter Seven

Conor stared at the dirty dishes on the table. He didn't need a fancy schoolteacher telling him how to run his life. He should have told Virnie to stop coming long ago. Instead, he'd let his silly notions of—he slammed a mental door closed. He had no idea of anything beyond surviving this harsh land. But his reluctance to say a final goodbye to Virnie had undone all his hard work in teaching Rae to be fearless.

Rae tiptoed in and hovered at the door. "Pa, is Miss White mad?"

Mad as a woman alone on the prairie. Mad as a bull eating locoweed. "Rae, you can't let fear run your life. You have to face it and conquer it."

"Yes, Pa."

"Never let that dog see you're afraid."

"Yes, Pa."

"Now do the dishes while I get something."

"Yes, Pa."

He fled the house. He'd equip Rae to handle the dog. He found a length of wood and smoothed it into a thick bat. She had nothing to fear except her own thoughts. This bat would give her the idea she was strong. That's all it took. Believing in your own ability.

He returned to the house and gave it to her. "You carry this with you. When that useless dog comes running out, you wave this and yell. He'll leave you alone soon as he sees you aren't scared."

She took the length of wood and waved it.

"Think you can handle it?"

"Yes, Pa."

He sat and watched her swinging the bat back and forth, testing its use. "Rae, you know what it takes to survive out here, don't you?"

Her arms fell to her side. She looked at him and nodded. "Being strong."

"That's right. And what happens if you're weak?"

"The country kills you."

"So what are you going to be?"

She grinned. "I'm tough as can be. You'll see."

He pulled her to his lap. "Good girl." He tickled her.

She screamed with laughter and tried to wriggle away.

"Not too tough to be ticklish I see." He stopped tormenting her and they grinned at each other. She understood the necessity of survival. "You're a good kid."

"I know." She scooted away and retrieved the bat. Again she swung it back and forth. She seemed pretty intent on trying different stances and checking her swing from both the left and the right.

"Whatcha' doing?"

"Practicing so I'll be ready."

"Good girl."

Virnie watched for Rachael the next day, wondering if Conor would have said something to end their friendship. She waited as long as she could before she rang the bell. Surely, Conor wouldn't refuse to let her attend school.

As the children lined up in twin rows, Rachael scurried down the road then slipped into place.

"Good morning, Rachael. I was afraid you might be late."

"Morning, Miss White," she murmured.

But though Virnie waited, Rachael refused to look directly at her, staring instead at the ground in front of her.

Virnie felt a great wave of disappointment but perhaps Rachael was only uncomfortable about being late. As the children had filed in, she wondered if it was more. Rachael scurried past Virnie without glancing up. Her shoulders were halfway to her ears and she twisted sideways as if she felt she had to protect herself from the teacher.

Virnie sighed quietly. Whatever Conor had said it had effectively created a barrier between herself and Rachael. It shouldn't matter so much. She'd done what she could to help Rachael and that should be enough. But it wasn't. She felt as alone as she had when she was a child. She forced her thoughts back to instructing the children before her.

At recess, Hilda hung back until all the others had left. "Miss White, I think you should look at Rae's leg." She hurried out before Virnie could question her.

Tiny little skitters of worry skipped along her nerves as she went outside to supervise the children. As she stepped out, Rachael fled to the far corner and displayed a devout interest in the grass.

Virnie circled the yard innocently as if interested only in what the children did. As she neared the corner, Rachael skipped away, headed for the outhouse. Virnie followed more slowly and waited nearby. But recess time was over and Rachael did not come out.

Virnie signaled to Hilda. She met her a few feet from the outhouse and whispered, "Ring the bell and get the children into their seats. Tell them to work quietly."

Hilda nodded and soon after the bell sounded. The children marched inside.

Virnie waited. Rachael would have to come out soon.

Sure enough. She heard the hook clatter. The door cracked open as Rachael peeked out. Virnie stayed out of sight until Rachael stepped to the dusty ground and reached down to fiddle with the bottom of her pants. Virnie could see she was trying to fold the edge to hide a bloodied tear.

Virnie clenched her teeth together. Why did Rachael hide an injury from her? Did she think it would make her weak to take care of it? She reached the child before Rachael noticed her. "I'd like to have a look at that."

Rachael jerked away. "It's nothing."

"Then I don't suppose there's any reason I shouldn't see it." She caught Rachael's arm gently, making it impossible for her to run away, and bent to lift the pant leg. A flap of skin gaped with ragged edges. Blood oozed into her sock.

Virnie bit her lip. Tears stung her eyes. Rachael must be in pain. And the wound needed attention. "Come to the cloakroom and I'll clean this up."

Rachael whimpered.

They paused at the schoolroom door. Virnie bent over to be eye level with the child. "Rachael, what happened?"

She shook her head.

"You must tell me."

"I can't. It's my fault."

"Come on. I'll see what I can do." She led the child into the cloakroom and left her on the narrow bench while she went to her desk and found a clean hanky. "Children, I am leaving Hilda in charge while I take care of something. George, you can borrow my grade nine text and see how many of the arithmetic problems you can do." She filled her cup with water from the pail at the back of the room and returned to Rachael. "Honey, this is a serious wound. I don't think you caught it on a fence or nail." There was another possibility. One that filled her stomach with such heaviness she felt ill. Tictoc, the ugly dog. She waited, hoping Rachael would choose to reveal the truth.

She washed the wound as well as she could but it needed to be disinfected and bandaged and she didn't have the supplies. She made a mental note to buy some things and keep them on hand. She tried to be gentle but Rachael quivered. Her eyes pooled with tears. White pinched the corners of her mouth. In fact, she looked like she might faint or throw up.

Virnie grabbed a sweater left on one of the hooks, scrunched it on the bench. "Put your head down here until you feel better."

The fact that Rachael did so without arguing

about how strong she was and how she didn't need help indicated how much she hurt.

Virnie sat on the floor stroking Rachael's forehead, waiting for the pain and weakness to pass before she pressed Rachael for more information. When the child's color improved she cupped Rachael's chin. "It was that dog, wasn't it?"

Rachael shook like hit by a strong wind and she choked back a sob.

Virnie sat on the bench and pulled Rachael to her lap. She pressed the child's head to her shoulder and held her tight. "It's all right. It's all right. You're safe now. I won't let him hurt you again. I promise." This was Conor's fault and his responsibility to make it better.

.Rachael sobbed quietly for several minutes and clung to Virnie.

Virnie continued to soothe her. Poor little girl. Trying to be tough in a situation too big for her to deal with.

Rachael quieted. She tipped her tear-stained face back to look at Virnie. "You mustn't tell Pa."

"I can't promise that."

"I told him I'd be strong. He'll think I'm not fit to survive on the farm." She shuddered. "Maybe he'll send me away."

Virnie's insides swept empty at the words. She'd been sent away. Yes, it was for the best and she had no regrets. But it still hurt. She pressed Rachael's head back to her shoulder so she wouldn't guess at the pain that washed over and over Virnie. She forced herself to take slow, deep breaths.

Forget the past. You're a lady now and someday you'll be a fine teacher.

Slowly, with a struggle that shredded secret, forbidden parts of her heart, she pulled herself under control. "I'm sure he won't send you away." But he must face a few hard truths as well. And Miss Virnie White was just the person to dish them out. She had nothing to lose. It wasn't like he was the answer to her maidenly dreams or anything. Not that she had such dreams, although she had gotten lost at his house, for a little while, in the fantasy of family and home. But no more. She intended to imitate Miss Price and be a dedicated teacher the rest of her life, helping hundreds of children. She ignored the ache edging those thoughts.

Certainly, if she had any lingering hopes of something besides being a spinster teacher they wouldn't include the likes of Conor Russell with his harsh outlook.

"You stay here and rest while I look after the rest of the children."

When Rachael curled up without protest, Virnie studied her with concern. It wasn't like Rachael to admit even a hint of being needy. Perhaps it was only the shock of the attack and her pain, but Virnie would be keeping a close eye on her until school ended and she could escort her home.

She'd arranged for someone from town to take them to the Russell farm in a wagon. Rachael's leg had swollen during the afternoon and she could barely walk. As soon as she got the child home, Virnie intended to start hot compresses.

She had the driver carry Rachael to her bed. She settled the child, elevating the injured leg on a pillow before she hurried to heat water. She'd seen Epsom salts in a cupboard when she cleaned and she dug them out and found an old towel that would do for making the pad.

She was stirring the salts into the water when Conor stomped in. "What's going on?"

"Sit down. We need to talk."

He shot her a startled look then obeyed.

She sniffed. Even a grown man didn't argue with Miss White, the teacher, at her finest. "I warned you about that dog. Rachael told you how afraid she was. What did you do? Give her a stick and tell her to be brave?" Rachael had told her everything on the ride home. The driver of the wagon had used his whip to repel the dog.

"Should be shot," he muttered.

Virnie couldn't help but agree. She was tempted to do it herself but there was something equally important to do here—convince Conor it wasn't weakness to need help or protection.

"The dog is all bluff," Conor said. "Rachael can handle him."

"That dog bit her. Badly."

He jolted to his feet. "How badly?"

"Tore her leg but she's fortunate it wasn't her face. Or her stomach."

"Where is she?"

"I'm not finished."

He scowled at her. "I don't need—"

"Maybe you do. No child should have to prove herself to her father."

"Maybe I was wrong about the dog. But it doesn't mean I think Rachael has to prove anything."

He breathed as hard as she. "She's small and defenseless. But it doesn't mean she's not of any value."

He stared at her for a moment, as though realizing she'd let something slip.

"I didn't say it did. Now where is she?" He headed for Rachael's bedroom.

Virnie sucked in air and prayed for strength. She'd failed to make her point clear. Her past got all tangled up with Rachael's situation. Then she followed him to the bedroom.

"Pa, I'm sorry. I tried my best."

"I didn't think he'd bite." He examined the gash then straightened and turned away, his face twisted with sorrow. "I'll take care of that dog." He strode from the room.

Virnie followed.

He paused to face her, bleakness drawing the skin tight across his face. "Will you tend to her while I'm gone?"

"Of course."

"That dog will not threaten her ever again."

Conor did not need the accusation in Virnie's eyes. He had enough from his own thoughts. What was wrong with him? He'd failed as a father to protect his child. He'd been so busy teaching her to be strong that he neglected to take into account the limitations of her size. Being small shouldn't be a cause for neglect. And that's exactly what he'd done. He'd given Rae no protection and certainly no tenderness. And he knew why. He'd given both to Irene and it hadn't been enough to make her survive the harsh winter. So he'd swung the other way. Indirectly, he was making Rae pay for her mother's weakness. Well, no more.

He rode into the Faulks' yard. The ugly, old mutt raced out and tried to bite Noble's heels. Conor was ready with a whip and caught the dog on the nose. It backed away whimpering and crouched behind a fence snarling.

Mrs. Faulk came out wielding a broom. When she saw the dog already skulking away from Conor and his horse, she put the broom down. "How can I help you?"

"Devin around?"

"Out at the barn, I 'spect."

"Thank you." He remembered his manners and touched the brim of his hat. "Ma'am."

He found Devin sitting in the shade of the barn, his hat pulled over his eyes. The man jerked up with a snort when he heard Conor approach. Conor didn't bother with any niceties. "Your dog bit my little girl. He threatens her every day as she goes to and from school."

Devin began to sputter a protest.

Conor cut him off before he could form a word. "You get him out of here immediately. If I ever see him again, I'll shoot him. On sight." He yanked the reins away and loped toward home and his hurting daughter.

Back home, he grabbed the saddle off Noble and hung it over the fence. He'd put it away later. And he'd brush Noble extra well later to make up for turning him loose with no more than a pat on the rump.

He threw back the door to the house and strode to the bedroom where Virnie sat on the side of the bed, tending a poultice on Rae's leg. "How is she?"

She nodded toward the door and followed him into the other room. "I'm concerned about the swelling.

And she's restless. I expect she's in pain but too brave to let us know. Did you take care of the dog?"

"I refrained from shooting it on sight, if that's what you mean. But I warned Devin if I ever see the dog again I will. I should have done it long ago. Just like I should have listened to Rae when she said she was afraid."

"It's all right to be afraid sometimes. In fact, it might be the smartest thing we can do in certain situations."

He shrugged. He didn't know about that but he had been wrong about making Rae so tough. "I have to talk to her."

Not caring that Virnie heard every word, or maybe glad she did so she would know he'd changed, he sat on the edge of Rae's bed. "I am so sorry I didn't listen to you when you told me about that animal. If I had this would never have happened."

"I'm sorry, Pa. I tried to be strong and brave like you said."

"You were very brave. But you shouldn't have had to be. It's my job to protect you from things that are too big for you. I will try not to fail you again. You have my word on it. But I need your word on something, too." He ignored Virnie's barely audible gasp. He didn't blame her for thinking he was about to make some impossible demand on Rae. He'd given both of them plenty of cause to think he didn't know how to be understanding.

"I'll try, Pa. Whatever you want me to do."

"Good. Because you'll face more scary things in the future, but I want you to promise me you will come to me when something is too hard for you. That way I can help you."

Her smile flashed and her eyes shone with love. "Pa, I promise."

He hugged her. She was so precious to him. How could he have put her at such risk because of his need to eliminate weakness from his life?

Virnie squeezed his shoulder.

Suddenly, his world felt whole and good—apart from Rae's injured leg.

He set Rae back on the pillow and stroked her head until she fell asleep. Both he and Virnie tiptoed from the room.

She turned to face him, her eyes glowing. "That was wonderful. You made her feel so special."

"I never meant to make her feel any other way."

"I understand that but sometimes a person's expectations of another can make them feel a failure."

He studied her, saw something dark in her eyes, something that went beyond his mistakes with Rae. He wondered if she'd had personal experience. "Do you know about this firsthand?"

Her expression switched to bleak and then to the mask of a professional teacher so quickly he blinked.

"This is about you and Rachael."

It might be but he wanted to know more about her. "Someday maybe you'll choose to tell me what makes Virnie White tick?"

She jerked around and seemed suddenly very interested in checking the pot she'd prepared for the poultices, moving jerkily as if controlled by an unseen puppeteer.

Sensing if he pushed too hard she would leave, he let the subject drop. "Would you mind staying around to help with her this evening?"

Her hands paused from their restless activity. She seemed to consider the idea then she slowly lifted her head and faced him, her eyes revealing nothing but calmness. "I'd be glad to help and make sure she's going to be all right. Would you like me to make supper?"

He held her gaze a moment without speaking, searching for the secrets she kept locked inside. But she allowed him no access. "I won't say no to such an offer."

Later, they sat beside Rae as she slept restlessly, moaning often and rolling her head back and forth.

"What's wrong?" he whispered to Virnie.

"I suppose she's reliving the fear and of course, her leg is painful."

He groaned. "I wish I could trade places with her."

She nodded. "None of us can change the facts, can we?"

There didn't seem to be a need to answer the question.

"Conor, can I ask you something?"

"Certainly."

"Have you ever regretted that Rachael is a girl?"

"Huh? What do you mean?" It was hard for him to guess what she felt as they whispered back and forth and when he turned to study her, she ducked her head.

"Have you wished she was a boy?" They hadn't lit a lamp, not wanting to waken Rae and even though Virnie watched him, he couldn't make out anything in her dark eyes.

"I have never regretted one thing about Rae. Not from the time she was born. She made her appearance in the middle of the night on a blustery October day threatening an early storm. I loved her so much it frightened me at first." He thought about that. "Maybe that's why I tried to make her strong. You know, so I wouldn't be tempted to coddle her. I learned my lesson with Irene on that matter."

"Not everyone is like Irene."

He nodded. "I think I'm learning that." He wished he could say more—something that would erase the tension in Virnie's expression—a tension that might be partly about Rae but he knew it went beyond Rae to something deep inside.

He could only hope she would tell him about it at some point. Because, he admitted, he cared how she felt.

Somehow, learning to admit that Rae had needs allowed him to think of caring about a woman who had weaknesses.

He turned away as confusion raced through him. Taking care of a child who was small and sometimes powerless in no way meant it was safe to trust a weak woman. And he would do well to remember it before he invited pain and disaster into his life again. Except it wasn't that simple. Virnie had done things that proved she had strengths. The way she handled the sick bull left him floundering to maintain his excuse that women were too weak for his kind of life. His insides bounced back and forth between protecting himself and Rachael from the hurt of depending on a weak woman and the evidence that said Virnie was different.

In the end, he could only allow himself to admit she was complicated. Didn't fit into any picture he had of a woman. Acknowledging it only increased his confusion.

Chapter Eight

Virnie wanted to stay and make sure Rachael was going to be all right. But she needed to get back before dark, before people could question her honorable intentions, so she made sure Conor understood how important it was to keep warm compresses on the wound. She prayed the swelling would subside and there would be no infection—the worst thing they could deal with.

She continued to pray as she walked to town, for Rachael and Conor and herself. She needed divine help sorting out her confusion.

Fear dried her mouth as she neared the Faulk place but no dog threatened her. At least she had accomplished something if she'd helped eradicate that danger.

She paused long enough to greet the Maxwells. She'd asked the wagon driver to let them know she would not be back for supper and now she explained about Rachael's injury then she retreated to her room and a chance to think.

Conor loved Rachael and had since the day she was born.

Had Virnie's father ever loved her? Maybe before her mother died? She didn't know.

Conor didn't care that Rachael was a girl.

Her father had clearly stated he wished otherwise for Virnie.

She jerked her thoughts to a halt. Why was she comparing Conor and her father? Her feelings toward Conor had nothing to do with her father.

Or did they? She studied the thought. She yearned for her father's love and acceptance. What did that have to do with Conor?

She faced the truth. She was angry at how he pushed Rachael to be strong but the feeling alternated with a lonesome yearning to share his love—like the obvious way he showed it to Rachael.

When he'd hugged the little girl, she'd instinctively clasped his shoulder, wanting something that could never be hers from either Conor or her father—acceptance, belonging, loving.

Yet briefly, as father and daughter hugged, she could not deny herself a taste of it.

Sharing their love, feeling it was temporary and she'd eventually go back to being Miss White, an admirable and devoted teacher.

But not until Rachael was better.

* * *

Rachael was not in school the next day nor did Virnie expect her. It would take a few days for her leg to heal.

Please, God, let it heal without infection, she prayed.

She'd promised Conor she would check on Rachael as soon as school let out. Never before had a day seemed so long. She thought dismissal time would never come. As soon as the last child scampered off, she closed the school without bothering to sweep the floor or clean the chalkboard. She'd arrive early tomorrow and do it. For now, she couldn't wait to see how Rachael was.

She alternately walked and ran the three miles to the farm, not caring that anyone seeing her would think it unsuitable behavior for a schoolmarm.

As she approached the yard, she noticed the stillness. No childish chatter, no sound of Conor working on the barn. Even the animals were quiet.

Her heart in her throat, fearing the worst, she tiptoed into the house and crossed to Rachael's room. The child lay on her back stroking Tippy. Relief flooded her to see Rachael looking pale but clear-eyed. "Where's your pa?"

"I don't know."

Anger chewed up her relief. Had he left the child alone? She turned and left the room. Her gaze swept across the space. She glanced into Conor's room. He lay sprawled facedown across the bed, his boots still on, looking like he had collapsed of sheer exhaustion. She returned quietly to Rachael's bedside. "He's sleeping. Did he stay up all night with you?"

"I don't know. I can't remember."

"How do you feel?"

"My leg hurts."

"Can I have a look?"

Rachael shrugged.

Virnie folded back the compress. The swelling had gone done a little but it still didn't look good. The edges of the wound showed a slight redness. "We need to keep hot compresses on this." She headed for the kitchen to prepare more salt solution.

As she placed the fresh compress on Rachael's leg the bed in the other room creaked and Conor moaned.

Virnie's heart stalled. She wasn't ready to face him. All her self-talk last night had done nothing to erase a long lonesomeness. She'd tried to blame it on wanting something from her father he'd never given. But it had not served to convince her. It wasn't her father she ached for. She wanted to be part of what she saw in this home—love and belonging. Even telling herself Conor's expectations were unreasonable didn't end her longing.

Because no matter what she told herself, a part of her refused to believe it.

When Conor didn't appear, she relaxed. The longer he slept the better for him. And the better for her. Surely, with time, she could end this foolish mental weakness.

She grinned. Now who was despising weakness? She glanced at Rachael to see if she noticed her teacher grinning at nothing. Rachael slept again, the cat curled at her side, purring.

"What's so funny?" Conor stood in the doorway, his hair mussed, his eyes still full of sleepy confusion.

She giggled. "You. You look a little rough around the edges."

"I feel it, too."

"Come on. I'll make you coffee." She drew him from the room.

"Rae?"

"Sleeping. Her leg looks a little improved."

He sank to the nearest chair.

"Tough night?"

"She had a lot of pain. It was hard to deal with. And I could do nothing."

"You kept the compresses on so you did something." She waited for the coffee to boil then poured him a cup.

He grabbed her hand.

His touch gave new life to all the arguments she had worked so hard to put to rest. She should pull away but she couldn't. Not when she saw the desperate look on his face.

"If anything happened to her—" He choked out the words. "How could I ever forgive myself?"

Feeling his fear and guilt, she sank to the nearby chair and wrapped both her hands around his. "Conor, you have made mistakes. Don't we all? But you have given her the best thing any parent can give a child. You have given her your love."

His gaze clung to her. She let him search her eyes, let him find her comfort and appreciation. After a moment, he said, "How could I not love my own flesh and blood?"

"Not everyone feels that way. Not all fathers love their children." She wanted him to see how special his love was.

Still he held her gaze and still she let him.

"Your father didn't love you?" His whispered words blew through her mind with the vengeance of a tornado.

She jerked her hands free and bolted to her feet, turning her back to him as she stared at the cupboard, trying to force her thoughts to what she could prepare for supper. She could be frozen in a block of ice for all the ideas she managed to come up with.

His chair scraped on the floor. His boots thudded toward her.

She couldn't move. She couldn't think past the words that had never been voiced. They had circled her mind, filled her thoughts, directed her reactions but they had never been given sound. Sound had given them a power she didn't believe possible. They cut through her defenses. They mocked her high and noble ambitions. They cut away all her progress. She stood alone and afraid in the middle of the floor feeling as frightened as the day she'd huddled in the corner of her childhood home wondering why she was alone.

Conor touched her shoulder. "I didn't mean to hurt you."

She wagged her head back and forth, unable to speak.

He made a frustrated sound. "Seems I manage to hurt people without even trying. First Rae and now you."

The pressure on her shoulder increased and he slowly turned her to him. Not speaking a word, he pulled her into his arms and held her. "I'm sorry. So sorry. I wish I could change things."

She didn't know if he meant what he'd said or the lack of love from her father. It didn't matter. He couldn't change anything. No one could. She simply had to accept the facts of her life. Put her past behind her. She remembered how often Miss Price had told her that. Miss Price would be disappointed to see she'd let the past affect her like this. And Conor must despise her for her weakness.

She let herself rest against his chest one more

heartbeat. Two. Three. And then with supreme effort, gathered together her rigid strength, wrapped it around her like armor and stepped back. "Sorry about that."

"Really?"

"I shouldn't let such things upset me."

"I'm not sorry." He headed for the bedroom. "It felt good to offer comfort to someone." He ducked out of sight.

She stared at the open doorway. It almost sounded like he'd found her weakness a welcome chance to show his concern. She snorted. All she was doing was adding things she wanted to a kindly remark.

Rae slept. He was pretty certain that was a good thing. No reason for him to stand there watching her except he knew he'd shaken Virnie with his stupid comment about her father. But it was so obvious from what she said, though if he'd guessed her reaction he would have kept his big mouth shut. He didn't want to upset her.

Though—he grinned—if it meant she would let him hold her it wasn't all bad. He'd been demanding toughness of Rae and himself so long he'd forgotten how good it felt to enjoy a little weakness. It made people come together for mutual support and comfort.

Hmm. Maybe he'd been heading in the wrong direction all this time. Two together was a good thing. If one fell down, the other could help him up. If one got discouraged, the other could point out reasons to keep on.

Rae jerked awake and cried out. "Pa, it hurts."

Conor knelt at the side of the bed and cradled her. "It's a nasty bite from a nasty dog." It about killed him to think this was his fault.

Virnie rushed into the room. "What's wrong?"

"Her leg hurts."

Virnie lifted the compress. "I'll get a fresh one." She kept her face and voice expressionless but she shot him a look that said so much. She worried about Rae as much as he did.

It felt good and right to have someone to share his concern. He held Rae close as Virnie tended the wound. There was so little they could do and he felt a vast helplessness. Maybe it was wrong to expect Rae to face the challenges of pioneer life. But when he thought of the uncertainty of life back East and how he had so often faced homelessness he knew going back wouldn't make things any better. He could do nothing but pray. And he did. For the first time in two years. He prayed for his daughter's healing as he held her and comforted her.

Virnie stood at his side and whispered, "I made some soup. It's ready in the kitchen. Go and eat while I hold her."

He didn't realize he'd been kneeling at the bed-side so long. He shook his head.

She touched his shoulder, the warmth of her hand and her concern brushing the cold edges of his heart. "You need to keep up your strength. Besides, she'll be safe with me."

He nodded and stood. She was very close. Close enough he had only to raise his hand to grasp her elbow. "I'm not worried about her safety. I just don't want to leave her."

"I know." She edged him toward the door. "Go eat."

They were far enough away Rae couldn't hear them. Conor grabbed Virnie by both elbows and held on. "I'm afraid."

Her expression softened and she wrapped her arms around him and hugged. "I know."

He held her a moment, taking from her the same comfort he'd tried to offer her a short time ago. And then feeling foolish at his weakness, he broke away and went to the table to eat the delicious creamy vegetable soup.

She stayed until almost dark. "I must go."

He nodded. "Yes, you must."

"I wish I could stay."

"Me, too."

They studied each other, knowing something had shifted between them. For a second, he wondered what it meant and where it would lead. Then he dismissed the questions. Right now all that mattered was they offered comfort to each other. And until Rae was better, he needed it and craved it.

"I'll be back after school tomorrow." She shifted her gaze and pink flushed her neck. "If you want me."

"I'll be counting the hours. It's worse when I'm alone."

She brushed her hand over his arm and then slipped away before he could think what he wanted to do.

Virnie knew Conor turned to her for comfort only because of Rachael. As soon as the child was better, he'd realize he didn't need her and they would slip back into their roles—he the strong one who needed nothing, no one; she the weak female who somehow, despite her perceived weakness, managed on her own.

But until Rachael was better, Virnie would spare no energy on such thoughts. For three days the child's leg remained swollen. Then slowly the swelling began to subside. The wound began to heal though she would have a very ugly scar.

Virnie spent Saturday at the farm, doing the homemaker things that gave her so much satisfaction. She did the laundry, scrubbed the floors and made a chocolate cake hoping to tempt Rachael's appetite.

Rachael was allowed up for lunch though both

Virnie and Conor deemed it best she allow her father to carry her to a chair and ordered her to keep her leg elevated.

Virnie tried not to be nervous around Conor. But remembering how they had held each other made it difficult especially when he seemed to watch her. And every time she caught him looking at her he held her gaze for a moment then shifted away slowly. She guessed he was as confused about what happened as she.

"Pa," Rachael said. "Can we go to church tomorrow?"

"No." Conor blurted out the word in explosive surprise. "You won't be going anywhere until your leg is completely better."

"Aww." She shifted her gaze to Virnie. "Are you going?"

"I expect so." Though she hated to be away from Rachael any more than she had to be. Her gaze shifted toward Conor. Yes. She wanted to share her time with him, too, even though she knew it was only until Rachael was better. "Why?"

"I want to see Alice."

"Can I take her a message? Or better yet, why don't you make a card and write a letter?"

Rachael brightened up at that.

Conor squeezed Virnie's hand. His silent approval filled her with a warm glow.

He went out to work and Virnie set up paper and

a pencil for Rachael who drew a picture of Tippy and wrote a note before she agreed to go back to bed.

While Rachael slept, Virnie continued to work. The sound of pounding came from the barn and she paused often to stare that direction. Occasionally she glimpsed Conor swinging a mallet or carrying a piece of lumber.

She jerked her gaze back to the basket of dry laundry. Admitting her attraction to Conor scared her. Especially given how he viewed weakness. Why would letting herself care about Conor be any different than caring for her father—she was bound to disappoint him, and she knew too well the pain of rejection.

As she ironed clothes, her back to the door, Conor stomped in. "Where's Rae?"

"Sleeping." She concentrated on removing the wrinkles from a shirt Rachael wore to school often.

"She is on the mend, isn't she?" His voice sounded almost directly behind her, sending shivers of warning up and down her spine.

"I would say so." She folded the shirt neatly and turned to pick up another item to iron.

His hand caught hers. She jerked to look at him as alarm sent her heart into a frenzy.

"I have never said a proper thank-you."

"It's not necessary." Her words practically stuck to her dry tongue.

"I think it is." He continued to hold her hand, slowly tugging her closer.

She pulled her hand away, pressing it to her waist and backed up until she encountered the ironing board. Her eyes felt several times too wide for her face.

He sighed and scrubbed his hair. "Virnie, why are you so afraid?"

"I'm not afraid of anything."

"I don't know what happened between you and your pa, but I am not your pa." He closed the distance between them as he spoke.

Anger boiled up inside Virnie. Was she so transparent that he saw her pain, her need? She wouldn't let it be so. Nor did she thank him for rekindling feelings she had put to rest years ago. "I am not comparing you to my pa." The guilt of her lie brought heat to her cheeks. "Why would I?"

He stood only a few inches from her, so close she could see the variation of blue-green in his irises and the white fan lines by his eyes from squinting in the sunshine. "You don't have to be afraid of me."

She shook her head, glancing past him in the hopes of finding escape. He blocked her so there was none. She grabbed the only safe subject she could find. "I'm glad for Rachael that you are willing to change how you treat her. She deserves to have her fears and weaknesses acknowledged."

"I know that. Maybe we all do. I know I'm changing how I view life."

"Good." She pushed past him and headed for the door with no idea of what she intended to do except escape.

But the man wouldn't take a hint. "Virnie, why are you running?"

She spun around to face him. "You misunderstand me. I am only concerned with Rachael."

His eyes darkened. His jaw clenched. "Of course. Like I said, I appreciate it."

He grabbed his hat and slipped past her to cross the yard and disappear into the barn.

She closed her eyes. She'd succeeded in deflecting his questions about her papa, and she'd managed to indicate her interest in being here was solely because of Rachael. It should feel good and right.

Instead it filled her with confusion and a disappointment that sucked at her insides.

It was three more days before Conor decided Rachael could attend school but only because he would personally give her a ride to and from. Every day, he waited until Virnie met his eyes before he nodded and rode away. He seemed disappointed with the way she remained distant and aloof. But she expected disappointment sooner or later so there seemed no reason to feel its sting so sharply.

Once Rachael was well enough to attend classes, Virnie told herself she would no longer go to the farm, but seeing Rachael's exhaustion at the end of the day, she knew the child could not cope with any more responsibilities. She managed to stay away until Saturday, then at Rachael's pleading promised to visit again. She fully intended to do more than visit. She would clean the house and do all the things Rachael couldn't possibly do.

And if she weren't such a coward she would explain her past to Conor. Then he would perhaps understand why she couldn't let herself trust a man to understand her needs.

Chapter Nine

Rae's injury had caused Conor to lose a lot of time rebuilding his barn. Not that he resented it. He was only happy her leg had healed and she seemed as good as new.

As he and Virnie worked together caring for Rae, he allowed himself to think of sharing his concerns and worries. He'd even thought the two of them would be stronger together. But she made it clear she wasn't interested.

He kicked himself all the way across the yard. He'd wasted far too much time thinking about the schoolmarm.

He stared at the remaining rafter he wanted to remove in the sod barn so he could build a nice frame structure. The sod one had served well but it was time for something better.

In the six years he'd been here, he'd done reasonably well. The good years balanced out the bad ones. He'd avoided going into debt and that had paid off. Life was good.

He grabbed the overhead rafter and tested it. Seemed loose already and he hadn't even removed any spikes. Probably had started to rot. He checked one end and found it solid.

Yes, it was a good life. He had everything he wanted. Everything. He clenched his fists. He had Rae, a solid house and he'd soon have a solid barn. He didn't need anything else. He certainly didn't need anyone to share his life, his concerns. Nor anyone to offer comfort.

He gritted his back teeth as an unwanted memory of Virnie holding him flashed across his mind. He forced the memory away, pushed aside the feeling of restfulness it had given him and marched to the end of the rafter. He shook it. Dirt sifted from the sod roof. This end was definitely loose. He'd have to brace it before it collapsed. He turned, intent on finding something sturdy enough for the task. A clump of dirt hit him in the shoulder. He glanced upward just in time to see the rafter give way and the roof fall. He lifted his arms to protect his head as the roof fell on him, pushing him to the ground.

Dirt stung his eyes, filled his lungs but he was alive. He coughed and sputtered and tried to move. He couldn't. The weight of the roof pushed him to the ground. The rafter pinned him. He could barely breathe as sod and dirt covered him. His neck felt as if something crawled across it. Spiders. He wriggled his fingers but couldn't move an arm to brush them off. He shuddered. No wonder Virnie hated and feared them.

He shifted his shoulders, squeezed his arm muscles, filled his lungs as much as he could in the filthy air and pushed. More dust sifted across his face. He held his breath to keep from inhaling it, but apart from the dust, nothing moved. His lungs hurt. He struggled to fill them but the rafter pressed against his chest. He grunted, sucked in air that tickled his lungs and made him cough. "Help." But who would hear him? He was alone apart from Rae who was still asleep when he left the house.

Sweat soaked his armpits, beaded on his forehead, pooled in his ears and tickled his neck. He shuddered, hoping the tickle came from sweat and not from creepy crawlies.

He struggled a few more minutes but it left him weak. He couldn't get in enough air. He lay still and tried to think what to do. His options proved mighty slim.

No one knew he was here.

No one would even miss him. Rae was used to him being away.

No one knew where he was.

No one would worry that he was missing.

Panic laced through him, making his lungs work even harder.

He forced himself to calm down. One person knew he was here. An all-seeing, all-knowing, all-loving God. A God he had neglected since Irene died. He'd blamed God for failing to keep Irene alive even as he had blamed Irene for her weakness.

Somehow it seemed wrong, weak even, to want God to help now when he hadn't given God more than a passing thought except for the time he prayed over Rae. But he could ask no one else for help. And no one could help him better. He knew that. There was a time he'd sought God more often. He'd trusted God to lead him to this homestead. He'd trusted God during his first Dakota winter when the cold and snow proved such a challenge.

God, forgive me for turning from You. I know I shouldn't have waited for a time such as this to turn back to You but better late than never. Help me. Send someone to rescue me. Like Gabe. He hasn't been here for a long time. About time he paid me a visit. Maybe Virnie might visit but she wouldn't be much use. A weak little thing. And scared of spiders.

He coughed as dirt tickled his throat.

Help me, God.

The blackness of his world blanketed his mind.

Virnie waited until after lunch to go to the Russell farm. She'd used the time to do her personal laundry, write a letter to Miss Price and grade some papers. Mostly she was forcing herself to exercise self-control. She would resist the urge to run to the farm simply to prove she could.

She walked along the road enjoying the late autumn. There had been several frosts and the morning air held a decided chill. Mr. Maxwell warned there would soon be snow.

But today was pleasant.

She found Rachael playing with Tippy apparently alone in the house except for the kitten. She refused to look about for Conor.

"How are you feeling?"

"Good. I'm hungry."

"Haven't you had lunch?"

Rachael shrugged. "I was waiting for Pa."

"You should know better than that. I'll make you a sandwich then you can help me make something for supper."

"Stew?"

"I think that would be good." There was some leftover roast that should be used up and Rachael could help peel vegetables.

Virnie tidied the house, then she and Rachael made a big pot of stew. By then the sun had almost slipped away. Virnie wanted to be home before dark but she didn't want to leave Rachael alone. "How long has your pa been gone?"

"He was gone when I got up this morning."

"Was he planning to go someplace?"

"Didn't say so."

"What's he been working on?" She'd managed to stay away for a few days and didn't know.

"The barn."

Alarm skidded across Virnie's shoulders and halted in her throat, making it difficult to swallow. What if he'd been hurt? She'd seen the size of the timbers he moved.

She forced her fear into submission and spoke calmly. "You stay here while I go look around."

Rachael nodded, distracted enough with the kitten to miss the worry in Virnie's voice.

Virnie stepped outside and called, "Conor?"

No answer but the sigh of the wind around the corner of the house. She studied the yard and surrounding area, hoping, praying, to see him headed for the house but saw nothing but shadows that suddenly seemed to vibrate with warning.

"Conor?" she called again as she crossed to the barn and stepped inside. But even the barn was filled with stillness. Where could he be? And why was she so worried? It wasn't unlike him to be away for long periods although he'd stayed close to home since Rachael's accident. Rachael was better now. No need to coddle her. Virnie knew that.

Her inner arguments did nothing to ease her concern.

Lord, is something wrong? Guide me.

She studied the inside of the barn. The roof was down at the far end where he'd been dismantling it to construct the new one. She considered the mess on the ground. Sods held together by yellowed roots lay scattered on the floor and heaped on the twisted remnants of rafters that had once been on the roof. The air was dank with the disturbance of old soil. She edged closer to examine the debris. Strange that he'd left it this way. She'd seen how careful he was about cleaning up after himself. Something important must have called him away.

She stepped over a pile of sod as she retreated. About all she could do was wait for him to return. Until he did, she would stay with Rachael. She couldn't leave the child alone even though she knew Rachael didn't seem to mind. She admitted it was as much for her sake as Rachael's that she decided to stay. Her insides knotted with concern. Perhaps it was only her imagination that made her fear something was dreadfully wrong.

She paused, called, "Conor?" even though she knew he wasn't here.

A sound came from a great distance. "Conor?" She raced outside to scan the surrounding landscape, saw no sign of him. Strange.

Something scratched at the back of her brain. Something she'd seen in the barn but not noticed. She retraced her steps. Noble stood in a pen watching her.

Noble. Conor's horse. Would he have gone to help a neighbor without riding his horse? Unless the neighbor had come in a wagon and Conor had ridden along. It was possible.

She stared at the horse and tried to sort out her confusion. Again she thought she heard Conor call from a great distance.

He had to be outside somewhere. She raced back into the dusk. "Conor?" she yelled. "Where are you?"

Again, no sign of a man striding toward her. She circled the barn, checking the shadows in case he had hurt himself and couldn't get up. Nothing. Nothing but emptiness.

Lord, are You trying to tell me something. Trying to guide me?

She stood stock still at the edge of the debris that had been the roof. She prayed for ears to hear the sound again, and a mind to know where it came from.

She strained to hear his voice. Her heart thudded loudly in her ears and she realized she'd held her breath so long her heart protested. She sucked in air and held it as she again listened with all her might. She heard the distant sound. This time she did not move. "Conor?" she called and waited for the sound to repeat.

It came again. Almost at her feet. Could it be? She shuddered from head to toe. Goose bumps

skittered along her arms. No! Not under there. She
backed away. Had she stood on him? Perhaps done
him damage? No. She couldn't think he was buried
beneath that debris. But the sound came again. She
was certain from under the pile of dirt.

She skirted the edges. How was she to get him
out? She could inadvertently do more harm than
good.

Her mind sprang to action on one front while a
second front stared in shock.

Light. She needed to see to do this right. She
glanced about and saw the lantern he'd hung on a
nail by the door. She raced for it, lit it and held it
out to pile of dirt. From the far end there protruded
a square rafter. She set the lantern on the floor and
lay down beside it to look under the rafter. She could
see nothing but more sod and eased out piece after
piece, exposing more of the beam. Dirt fell into
her face and she sputtered. She reached farther
beneath the rafter, felt something different. Fabric.
She peered into the hole. Definitely fabric but she
couldn't pull it free. Could it be part of Conor's
clothing? "Conor?"

"Here," came a harsh whisper.

Her heart exploded against her chest and she
gasped. "Thank God. Can you move?"

"Pinned by wood." He sounded in pain,
befuddled.

"I'll get you out." She sat back on her heels to

collect her thoughts and come up with a plan. She couldn't move the beam. It was too heavy by itself but now covered in sod…impossible for her to manage on her own and there were no sturdy men around to help. She knelt to speak into the hole. "I'll have to move the dirt off you first and then lift the beam."

"Spiders."

She shuddered. "I'll deal with them later." They didn't matter as long as Conor lay buried. She lifted clumps of sod, careful as to where she stepped aware she could increase the pressure on Conor, perhaps suffocate him. She cleaned away inches at a time, trying to make a path parallel to the beam. Slowly she exposed it. Inch by inch she revealed his face, black with dirt, his eyes like white discs.

"Water," he croaked.

She dashed for the well and pumped a dipper full and carried it back. She edged as close as she could and held the dipper to his mouth. Much of the water ran down his neck leaving muddy tracks but he sucked in enough to ease his discomfort.

"Can you slip out now?"

"I'm pinned at my knees. I can't feel them. Maybe my legs are cut off."

She managed to stifle her gasp and hide her alarm. "I need to check before I move anything else." If his legs had been severed and she released the pressure of the beam he stood a good chance of bleeding to death.

She moved more clods of dirt. She freed one arm. "Your arm is free and whole."

"I can't feel it."

Might be a good thing. She couldn't begin to guess how damaged it was and how it would pain when feeling returned. "Don't move." She had cleared enough space for her to crawl in close to his shoulders and she carefully edged closer. She wanted to wipe the dirt from his face, smooth away his concern, but that would have to wait until he was safely out of this mess.

Lord, I don't know what I face. Guide my hands and give me wisdom.

"I'm going to reach down and see if I can determine what's going on with your legs." She slid her hand cautiously along the rough timber, found where it crossed his legs and then she could move no further. "I'll have to move more dirt. I know you're anxious to be out of here but I must move slowly and carefully."

"Spiders."

"I don't care."

"In your hair. Now."

She brushed her hands over her hair, hoping she'd dislodged any unwelcome visitors. She couldn't restrain an audible shudder.

"Sorry," he murmured.

"We'll discuss it later." Right now she had a task to do. Slowly, she eased the clumps of dirt off the beam, holding her breath each time, wondering if the beam would lift and he'd bleed to death before she could get to him.

Every few minutes, she felt along the wood to see if she could locate the rest of his legs. Inch by inch his body was exposed. Every time she saw more she sucked in relief when there was no massive amount of blood. She reached the area where the beam crossed his legs and hesitated. What she did next could mean life or death for Conor. She would not move until she had taken every precaution. She gathered together a length of rope in case she needed to secure the beam and some lengths of leather belting in case she needed to stop bleeding.

"I'm going to see what's under this pile."

He nodded, his eyes bleak, preparing himself for the worst.

Inch by dreadful inch, she moved the dirt until she could finally see his legs. They were intact. "Your legs are okay. All that's wrong is the beam is on them." How was she to get it off? If she rolled it, she would do more damage. She couldn't sling a rope over a rafter and lift it because there was no roof over their head. She stood and considered her options. What she needed was a way to raise it. One end protruded past Conor's head to solid ground.

The other lay across his feet. If she could lift the end at his feet…

She'd done something like this when she helped Miles with a wagon that needed to be lifted so he could replace a broken axle. "I'll be right back." She found a solid length of wood and some short chunks used to block the wheels of a wagon. She staggered back to the barn with them and fixed a lever. "I'm going to lift the beam off you. If you can drag yourself out that would be good." Otherwise she would have to find a way to secure it so she could drag him to safety.

"It's heavy."

"I can do it. I know how." But she didn't know how long she could hold it. Or if it would roll as she lifted it. "Be ready to move." She braced herself and raised herself over the length of wood. She wanted to lift the beam slowly. "On the count of three. One, two, three—" She threw her weight to the lever and the beam lifted.

Please, God, don't let it roll back on him. Please, God, give me strength.

Conor groaned but managed to drag himself far enough away that she could drop the beam. She hurried to him, running her hands along his leg. *Let there be no blood. Spurting blood.* His trousers were torn. There were plenty of cuts and scrapes but her worst fears were set to rest. "How do you feel?"

"I don't know. Grateful to be free." He struggled to sit, his arms seeming unable to push him upright.

She helped him up. "Take your time."

"Aggh. My legs are coming back to life. Aggh."

She knew he wouldn't be able to walk but she needed to get him to the house. With his help, she managed to drag him across the yard. At the door, she hesitated. "I think I'll tell Rae to go to her room."

"She's tough." He grunted. "But I don't want her to see me like this."

"I'll be right back." She made sure he was steadied against the wall then slipped inside.

Rachael bounced from the chair where she'd been playing with Tippy. "Pa?"

"I found him. He'll be here in a minute." She tried to think of a way to persuade Rachael to go to her room without alerting her to Conor's condition. "Why don't you surprise him by brushing your hair and putting in those pretty hair ribbons?"

"Aww. He doesn't care about that sort of thing."

She was right on that score. "Then do it for me. I like to see your hair pretty."

"Okay."

Virnie waited until Rachael ran to her room, then quietly closed the bedroom door behind her hoping she would be too busy brushing her hair and playing with the cat to give it a thought.

She returned to Conor and helped him scoot across the floor. She aided him to his bed before Rachael rushed out of her room. "Pa?"

Virnie slipped out, closing the door behind her. "Rachael, your pa's had an accident. He's all right, just a little dirty but I think he'll need us to be quiet tonight."

Rachael headed for the bedroom door. "Pa?"

"Come in," Conor called.

Virnie followed the girl into the room.

Rachael skidded to a halt. "What happened to you?"

Virnie answered for Conor who looked about ready to pass out. "He was working on the barn and the roof fell on him." She still couldn't believe he was safe, that his legs hadn't been severed. Though it was too early to tell if they had been damaged.

She let Rachael check him out for a few minutes as she prepared a basin of warm soapy water. The first thing he needed would seem to be a good scrubbing. And water to drink.

She helped him lift his head and held a cup to his lips. He eagerly sucked back the water, panting with exhaustion when he finished. She held her hand behind his head a second longer than necessary, wanting to wrap her arms around him and hold him close. She couldn't believe he had escaped in one piece.

"I'm going to wash off some of the dirt now."

He made a noise she took for agreement but didn't open his eyes.

She dipped her cloth into the warm water but hesitated. She knew performing this little task would cross a boundary in her mind. It would allow her to touch him at his weakest. It would make her feel as if she gave him strength. And that, she understood, would bind her forever to him in her thoughts.

But she had no choice. She couldn't leave him untended. And she couldn't deny the ache in her heart to wash the dirt from his face and see the man—

She wouldn't finish it. She wouldn't admit she had grown to love him. Her heart felt like it ripped down the center—one half wanting to love him, the other full of warning.

She washed his face, unable to stifle the tender feelings as she saw the bruises. She wiped blood from scratches and saw the tension around his mouth. "Are you in much pain?"

His eyes snapped open for a second. She gasped at the darkness in them. "How much is much?" His voice grated.

"I'm sorry. I wish I could do something."

"You did."

Shock hit her with the suddenness of falling down

an endless flight of stairs. He could have died. It was a miracle he didn't. "How long were you there?" she whispered.

"What time is it?"

"Almost nine. At night."

"I went out right after breakfast. Wasn't long after."

"You must have been there almost twelve hours. It's a miracle you didn't suffocate."

"It's a miracle my legs aren't cut off." He caught her gaze and held it. "I prayed someone would rescue me. Didn't figure it would be you."

"Why's that?"

"It was a big job. And spiders." He shuddered. "They crawled all over me and I couldn't do a thing."

"Uggh. I would have gone crazy." She finished washing his face and hands. He needed to be checked for injuries. Her face heated like she'd bent over an open flame. She couldn't do it. After all she was the very proper Miss White—schoolteacher and example to the young ones. But who would perform this task? There were neighbors, of course, but how could she contact them?

She had no way to do so.

Lord, send help. Though she couldn't imagine how He would.

She returned to the kitchen and cleaned up the dirty water.

Rachael hung at her heels. "Pa's going to be all right, isn't he?"

"I believe so." She'd feel more confident if someone could examine his legs. For all she knew one or both could be broken. Her only consolation was the lack of serious amounts of blood.

Rachael grabbed the milk pail. "I forgot to milk the cow."

Virnie laughed. "You were waiting, hoping your pa would do it." He'd milked the cow since Rachael's accident. "I think you're getting a little spoiled." She never thought she'd see that day.

Rachael managed to look both embarrassed and annoyed. "I 'spect I have to do Pa's chores, too, now."

"For tonight, certainly. He won't be going anywhere."

Rachael ducked out the door and Virnie returned to Conor's bedside. She had to watch him carefully for shock or signs of undisclosed injuries.

He opened his eyes and stared at her.

"Any change in how you feel?"

"Actually, I'm feeling a tiny bit better. Not quite so shaky." He coughed and his face twisted with pain.

She found him a hanky, not surprised to see he coughed up dirt. She helped him drink more water.

"Sit beside me."

She did so, uncertain if she should. But she couldn't pretend she didn't care deeply. Until she knew he would be fine…

"You surprised me."

She snorted.

"I didn't know you could be so tough…so resourceful."

"I learned to be as a child."

He reached for her hand.

His touch combined with her fear widened the securely barred door of her memories. She shivered as things from her past escaped, demanding acknowledgment. "I told you my mama died when I was young. I don't remember her." Sadness filled her at the vastness of her loss. She swallowed hard and gripped Conor's hand. "My brother was six years older. My pa—" She swallowed hard and forced back tears. "He didn't have use for a little girl. Told me I should have been a boy. He shifted me off to Miles. I followed him around and learned to do everything he did."

"If he's the one who taught you to be so resourceful, I'm awfully glad you did." He smiled, his gaze steady despite the underlying pain. "I'm awfully glad," he whispered.

"My pa gave me to Miss Price to raise when I was ten. I haven't seen him since. Nor Miles." An ache as wide as the endless sky sucked at her insides and tugged forbidden tears to the surface.

He reached upward with a hand and wiped a tear from the corner of each eye. "No wonder you didn't like how I was raising Rae. You thought it was a repeat of your father."

She nodded.

"It's not. I love Rae. I wouldn't trade her for a dozen sons."

"I know."

A spider crawled across the back of her hand and she jerked to her feet, screaming as she shook it off.

Conor laughed.

She scowled at him. "Nothing funny about the creepy things."

"Don't I know it?" He caught her hand and urged her back to his side. "Yet you paid no attention when you dug me out." His eyes revealed something beyond gratitude, something that held her heart in a gentle, reassuring grasp.

She couldn't pull away any more than she could hide her emotions. "There was something far more important to tend to." She managed to duck her head and hide her face lest he read all that was in her heart. She didn't want to face it any more than she wanted him to guess it.

Rachael returned to the house. "I'll go help her with the milk."

She made her anxious escape. As she helped Rachael she prayed for someone to come and help her and at the same time, fretted about how she'd manage if no one came.

Hoping for someone to come, she thought she heard the rattle of a wagon. She shook her head. Getting fanciful.

But Rachael raced to the door and peaked out. "It's Uncle Gabe and he's got a lady with him." She ran out the door yelling, "Uncle Gabe, Uncle Gabe."

Relief raced through Virnie. *Thank You, God.* She couldn't have asked for a better answer to her prayer. Gabe was Conor's friend.

She waited at the table for Gabe to enter, a young woman on his arm.

"What's this I hear about Conor?"

Virnie guessed Rachael had filled him in. "He's had an accident."

"He's in there?" Gabe tipped his head toward the bedroom and Virnie nodded.

"Gabe?" The young woman spoke softly.

"Oh, I'm sorry. Miss White, meet the new Mrs. Winston. I took Conor's advice and quit putting off our marriage until everything was in tiptop shape. Besides, my new wife assures me she'll help."

Virnie laughed at how Gabe rattled on. "He sounds a little excited," she said to his wife.

"Call me Diana and yes he's been talking nonstop for the past four hours. I keep thinking he'll run down but he shows no sign of it."

Gabe rolled his eyes. "I have not been talking that much."

Diana giggled. "If you say so."

Virnie liked the woman right away. Her pale brown hair was scooped up into a stylish roll. Her bright gray eyes were direct and dancing with humor.

"Gabe?" Conor's weak voice came from the bedroom. "That you?"

Gabe didn't move. "How is he?"

Virnie lowered her voice. "I haven't checked his legs. I'll let you do that." She ignored Gabe's chuckle as her cheeks warmed. "He's lucky to be alive and very fortunate to have both legs." She explained how she'd found him and dug him out. Gabe squeezed her shoulder and Diana took her hand.

"It sounds awful," Gabe said.

"You were very brave," Diana whispered.

"I only did what had to be done."

Gabe stepped toward the bedroom. "I'll have a look at him."

Virnie nodded gratefully, praying he would find Conor's legs intact. Suddenly her knees melted and she grabbed for a chair.

Diana patted her back. "We're here now. You'll be okay."

Virnie knew she'd be okay. But she'd never be the same.

Chapter Ten

Virnie waited with Rachael and Diana as Gabe stepped into the bedroom, closing the door behind him.

Virnie shuddered as she heard Conor groan. *Please, God. Let him be all right.*

Gabe came from the room. "I need soap and water."

He didn't say anything more as she handed him what he required. He just shook his head when she raised her eyebrows in silent inquiry. But his face set in hard lines as if he didn't like what he saw. He ducked back inside without easing her concern.

"I'll make tea." She needed something to occupy her hands as well as her mind.

The kettle boiled. She poured the water over the tealeaves and still Gabe did not return. She could hear the murmur of voices and wondered what transpired.

She sat across from Diana and tried to find something to talk about, something to divert her from worrying about Conor. She couldn't stop thinking he might have injuries she hadn't discovered. "When were you married?"

"Gabe came home a week ago. We married right away and packed up my things and here we are."

Virnie nodded. "Congratulations."

"How long have you been in the Dakotas?"

Virnie pulled her thoughts into some semblance of order. After all, she was the teacher and should be able to carry on a decent conversation. "I came out in September. I'm the schoolteacher."

Gabe stepped from the room again. He handed Virnie the basin and rolled down his sleeves.

She stood holding the basin, waiting for him to tell her. "Is he…?"

"There doesn't appear to be anything broken though he's badly bruised. Lots of cuts and scrapes but I don't think anything serious." He squeezed Diana's shoulders. His wife rested her cheek against one hand and covered the other with her palm, the tender gesture driving a deep ache to Virnie's heart.

Gabe shook his head. "I'm concerned there might be damage to his legs from being under such pressure for so long." He ground about on his heel. "What was he thinking to be out there without telling anyone? Does he think he's invincible? Well, he proved he's not." He paced to the door and back. "When I think…" He cast an eye at Rachael and didn't finish.

Rachael jumped to Conor's defense. "Pa's tough. He doesn't need anyone to take care of him."

Gabe squatted to face her. "Rae, we all need someone at some time. And what's this I hear about you?" He nodded toward her leg.

"A big bad dog bit me. I tried to beat him off with a stick like Pa said but this dog was really big and really bad." She lifted her pant leg to reveal the angry red scar.

Gabe examined it carefully. "Nasty bite."

"Wasn't nothing," Rachael said, eliciting a chuckle from everyone. When she glanced at Virnie she lost her braveness. "It hurt some but Virnie took care of me."

Gabe sank to one of the chairs. "I don't know about you Russells. It seems it's not safe to leave you alone. You need someone to keep an eye on you both." His gaze settled on Virnie.

"Don't look at me. I'm only the schoolteacher."

Gabe grinned. "And I would say you've taught them some valuable lessons about taking care of themselves and others."

His acknowledgment touched a tender spot close to Virnie's heart.

"Virnie." Conor's low voice came from the bedroom.

Virnie jumped to her feet and instantly regretted her hurry when Gabe laughed.

"Seems he's taught you to jump to his command."

She hesitated, twisting her hands, trying to find an excuse for her behavior.

Diana smiled. "Pay him no mind. He's only teasing."

Virnie still hesitated, flustered by Gabe's comment and alarmed at her own response. She ached to see Conor and to assure herself he was indeed alive and well.

"Go on." Diana waved toward the door. "You don't want him getting agitated."

She hurried across the room, well aware of the amused glances Diana and Gabe exchanged.

She stepped into the bedroom, leaving the door ajar. Conor wore a clean nightshirt and lay beneath the covers. She was pleased to note Gabe had made sure to tent the covers over Conor's toes to prevent pressure. It was too early to tell if normal feeling would return to his legs and feet.

"How are you?" What a stupid thing to ask but suddenly she couldn't get a clear thought into her head.

His forehead and right eye were even more swollen than she remembered. And so many cuts and bruises. One cut on his cheek oozed blood and she bent over to swab at it with a clean handkerchief.

He caught her hand and pulled it to his chest. Fearing he would see how she felt, she averted her gaze.

"Virnie," he whispered.

She couldn't stop herself from looking into his eyes. Dark blue and bottomless, pulling her deeper and deeper into his emotions. She saw past his strength, beyond his need to be independent, to the soft core of his heart where he longed for the same things as she—acceptance, belonging and understanding of secret weaknesses.

His gaze searched her deepest thoughts. Did he see the same things in her she saw in him? She realized with a start that she wanted him to. Wanted him to understand her weaknesses didn't make her unacceptable. They only made her need someone who understood, accepted them as a counterbalance to her strength.

He cupped her head and pulled her closer.

Aware of her deep longing and unable to exert caution, she responded to his urging until her face was inches from his. This close she could see dirt embedded in the lines of his face. She thought she had washed him better than that.

"Virnie, you saved my life. I will forever be grateful." He pulled her closer still.

She knew he meant to kiss her. Understood she had only to pull away to make it impossible. Instead, she closed her eyes and let him catch her lips in a gentle kiss.

He groaned and she jerked back.

"I think the inside of my mouth is cut." He ran his tongue around the inside of his lips then reached for her shoulder and pulled her to his chest.

She laid her head against his warmth, listening to the beat of his heart. "I'm so glad you're safe," she murmured.

"Umm." He stroked her hair.

For a moment she let herself bask in his attention. But her rigid self-control exerted itself. She could not allow her feelings to follow her heart without restraint. She sat up, remaining on the edge of his bed. "God has answered so many prayers today. I don't think I would have found you without His help and I prayed for someone to come and help us and Gabe shows up."

"I can't believe he up and married. He's talked about it for two years."

Virnie jerked to her feet. "You haven't met Diana yet."

He caught her hand. "I wanted a few minutes alone with you."

Her cheeks warmed and she knew they would signal her embarrassment. Only it was more pleasure than embarrassment.

"You aren't offended, are you?"

She snorted. "You remember me struggling to resist you?"

"No."

"Then I guess you have your answer."

He grinned—slightly off center because of the swelling in his face but the nicest sight she'd seen in some time. Well, since she'd found him safe and sound under the pile of dirt.

"I'll let Gabe introduce you to his wife." She returned to the kitchen. "He'd like to meet Diana," she said to Gabe.

Gabe pulled his wife to her feet. "Now don't you be feeling too sorry for him because of his injuries."

Diana's eyes sparkled with adoration of her husband. "I can feel sorry for him but don't think I'll ever see anyone else but you with any sort of specialness."

Rachael giggled as they went into Conor's bedroom. "They're silly."

"They're in love." Virnie cleaned up the basin and washed the tea things.

"Oh, you shouldn't have done that. I intended to," Diana protested as they returned to the kitchen.

Gabe yawned. "I expected Conor to invite us to stay the night. Guess I'll just have to invite myself." He glanced about. "We'll just bed down next to the stove." He nodded toward the corner stove in the sitting area of the room.

Rachael yawned.

Virnie realized how late it had grown. "Good thing there isn't school tomorrow. I should have sent you to bed long ago."

"Are you staying, too?" Rachael asked.

Virnie would love to just so she could know for certain Conor was fine. But the house was already crowded and the Maxwells would be wondering what happened to her. "I better get back home."

"I'll give you a ride," Gabe said.

She was so bone tired she couldn't refuse.

The next day was Sunday and she hurried to church, eager to pour out her gratitude to God over Conor's safety.

Rachael raced up to her as she reached the church steps. Diana followed at a more sedate pace.

"How is Conor today?" Virnie asked the other woman.

"Cranky. Gabe figures his legs are hurting. But he says feeling and movement are coming back." Gabe had stayed back at the farm with Conor.

Relief washed through Virnie followed by a wish she could be there to comfort Conor.

Diana smiled and leaned close. "He made me promise to bring you back with me."

Virnie nodded and looked away as if greatly interested in something at the far side of the yard. The way her pulse quickened and warmth flooded her eyes revealed far more than she wanted Diana to see. It was only because she was concerned with Conor's well-being, she firmly informed herself.

But she found it difficult to sit calmly through the service and after it ended, had to remind herself to introduce Diana to the others.

"I'm hungry," Rachael said.

Virnie welcomed the excuse to escape. She tried to still her anxious feet as they walked to the farm.

Diana laughed as Virnie's pace increased. "It's hard to be apart, isn't it?"

Virnie slowed her steps. "I'm not sure what you mean."

Diana chuckled. "I suppose it's possible you haven't yet figured it out."

Virnie knew what she meant but didn't want to deal with her emotions and certainly did not want to discuss them.

Conor sat on the chair with his right leg propped on a stool. Gabe, suddenly bossy and nurturing now that he was married, warned him he'd have to take care of his leg until it was back to normal.

"You're lucky you didn't lose it."

Conor sighed. "You think I don't know that?"

"I don't know what you know. You sure aren't as smart as I thought you were to get yourself trapped in the first place. You might have let someone know where you'd be."

"I didn't expect the roof to cave in."

"Good thing for you Virnie had the guts to dig you out."

Conor grinned. "Surprised me some. I wouldn't have thought she could get that beam off me."

Gabe tapped Conor's shoulder. "If you let that woman get away I will know for certain you are crazy."

Conor snorted. He didn't want to let her "get away" as Gabe so elegantly said. But what did Virnie want? He didn't know. Perhaps he could convince her she wanted to share his life. He looked forward to the challenge.

Gabe went out to check on the livestock, leaving Conor alone in the kitchen.

He watched the door. Rae and Diana should return from church soon. Diana had promised to do her best to bring Virnie with her.

He heard their steps and Rae laughing as they approached the house. His lungs stiffened with anticipation bringing on a bout of coughing. He held his breath, stifling the coughs so he could focus on the door.

Rae raced in. "Hi, Pa." She found Tippy sleeping near the kitchen stove and scooped up the growing kitten.

Diana entered next and glanced around. "Where's Gabe?"

"Went out to look after the horses."

She nodded and turned back to find her husband.

Conor waited. Was that all? And then Virnie stepped into the room and ground to a halt at seeing him sitting up. Her gaze darted to his leg as if to assure herself it was still there and then her dark eyes sought his and clung. He read her concern and let it pour into the resistant corners of his heart until he felt warm and full and satisfied.

Well, almost satisfied.

"You're up," she whispered.

"Gabe helped me."

"Your legs?"

"The right one is still a little unsteady but they both feel almost normal."

Air whooshed from her lungs and her eyes glistened. "I'm glad."

As if aware of how much she'd revealed, she turned toward the stove. "I'll make lunch."

He watched her bustle around the kitchen. More and more he realized how much he needed her. How his need made him stronger rather than weaker. How the two of them formed such a strong team. She was so skittery around him he figured he better move slowly.

The others returned and sat down to a simple

meal. Gabe rattled on about the mess he'd found at the barn.

Finally, Conor could take no more. "Look, I wasn't being careless. As soon as I realized the rafter was loose I prepared to brace it. It just came down before I could."

Gabe opened his mouth to argue.

Diana caught his hand. "Leave him alone, dear. I think you've made your point."

Gabe grinned at his wife. "You're right. How did I ever manage without you?" He turned to nod at Conor. "Married less than a week and I can already see how much I am going to benefit."

Diana rolled her eyes dramatically, causing Rae to break into giggles. "You only think being married means good meals and clean laundry."

Gabe choked. "I never said that."

Diana chuckled. "Then what did you mean?" Her eyes twinkled and Conor sat back and grinned, happy to see Gabe had found himself a woman would who keep him guessing.

Gabe realized she was teasing and sighed. "Woman, I can tell you will never give me any peace unless I confess it's a whole lot more than food and clean clothes." He bent close and caught Diana's chin. "You make me more whole than I've ever been."

Rae giggled more then sobered. "Uncle Gabe, how could you be more whole?"

"I don't know. I just know I am. It's like Diana here has taken things I didn't know were missing in my life and filled in the blanks."

Conor stared at his friend. "I would have never guessed you to be so…so…"

"Poetic," Diana said. "That was very sweet, Gabe. Thank you."

Virnie rose suddenly and busied herself with tea.

Conor watched. What was she thinking? He saw the tension across her shoulders. Did she find it hard to believe a man valued a woman like Gabe valued Diana? Her father had given her reason to doubt it. Guilt and regret dried his mouth. He'd not given her any reason to trust a man's opinion of a woman, either. Unintentionally he had equated her role as a teacher with weakness.

He sensed he had his job cut out for him in proving he didn't believe it any longer. She had more than adequately proven her strength.

And he wanted to share it with her. Maybe, like Gabe, her strength would fill in the blanks in Conor's heart.

Lord, You rescued me through Virnie when I was trapped. Now I seem trapped by my own reactions to Irene's death. Help me escape from them as well. And show Virnie that I value her in every way.

He hoped for a chance to talk to her privately but with so many people wandering around the house, practically tripping over each other, the afternoon passed without providing him an opportunity.

And then Diana and Virnie worked together to make supper. As soon as the dishes were washed, Virnie announced she had to get back home.

"I need to prepare some lessons and write some letters." Her eyes seemed to beg for something from Conor as she met his gaze across the table.

"If Gabe took you home, you could stay a little longer," he said.

"Yes, please do," Diana added. "Gabe won't mind taking you back to town, will you, dear?"

Gabe nodded, distracted by the game he and Rae played with the kitten, rolling a marble back and forth between them for Tippy to chase.

Virnie nodded. "Very well." She avoided looking at Conor.

He wished he knew what she wanted.

A little later, he yawned.

"You've had a long day," Virnie murmured.

Weariness suddenly made it difficult to think. "I think I'll call it a night."

Gabe jumped to his feet to assist him.

For a moment, Conor thought of refusing to drape his arm over Gabe's shoulders. He preferred to manage on his own. But he'd learned *alone* didn't make him strong. It only made him lonely. He grabbed Gabe's shoulders and hobbled to the bedroom. Gabe helped him to the bed.

"Thanks."

"How are your legs?"

"Sore."

"That's probably a good sign, wouldn't you say?"

"It's better than feeling nothing." They both knew the damage of his injuries could have cost him his legs.

Gabe stared down at him. "Do you need help getting into bed?"

"Do I look like an invalid?" He couldn't keep the edge of frustration from his voice.

"Nope. But you sound like one."

"Sorry. I'm tired."

Gabe backed away. "If there's nothing more you need…"

He needed to see Virnie and talk to her but he could hardly ask her to visit him in his bedroom. Yesterday following his rescue had been an extenuating circumstance.

Today was different.

Chapter Eleven

Virnie closed the school and headed down the road with Rachael. She'd gone to the farm every day this week. With Gabe and Diana there no one could complain it was inappropriate. But only because they couldn't see her thoughts. She ached for the minutes she spent at the farm. If only she and Conor could spend more time alone.

But what would that accomplish? She certainly wouldn't be blurting out that she just might love him a tiny, tiny bit. Besides, the idea churned around inside her like tumbleweed caught in a dusty twister. Loving a man, wanting his returning love was a dangerous thing. She shied away from the idea, afraid of being hurt. Yet she couldn't quite succeed at pulling her thoughts into denial.

The only way she kept up with preparation of her lessons was to rise early and do them before the children arrived. She'd written a letter to Miss Price the first of the week and reported on Conor's accident. At that point she'd paused as she sought for a way to explain how she'd felt at being able to rescue him. Finally she wrote, "It made me feel useful." She wished she could also say how it made her value the hard lessons she'd had before she went to live with Miss Price. But Miss Price had always insisted she must forget the past. In the end she chose to say nothing on the matter.

It was Friday and Virnie felt as if she had been given a long overdue holiday. It was about all she could do not to skip along the road as Rachael did.

"Aunt Diana is going to teach me to bake oatmeal cookies tomorrow," Rachael announced.

"That's nice." Virnie didn't know why she continued to go to the farm. It wasn't as if they needed her anymore. Diana made delicious meals and spent a great deal of time teaching Rachael how to manage.

Gabe looked after the chores.

Even Conor didn't need her. He hobbled about insisting his leg felt better with each passing day.

They approached the farm and Rachael ran ahead calling, "Pa. Pa." Conor sat in the sunshine beside the open door to the house.

Virnie's pace picked up without conscious decision on her part. Then she saw Gabe on the ground next to him and slowed. Maybe if they ever got a chance to talk…

But what did she expect from him? That he'd do more than express gratitude for her help which is what he'd done several times since the night of the accident. His kiss meant no more than that.

She almost stopped walking as she admitted the longing that had tugged at the edges of her mind for the past several days. She wanted so much more than gratitude.

She wanted acceptance, love and acknowledgment. Things she'd wanted all her life and never had. She ought to know better than to wish for them at her age. Shouldn't she have outgrown those childish wishes?

Conor called, "Hello."

"How are you today?" She asked the same thing every time she saw him as if there was nothing more to say between them.

"Better every day." He, too, said the same thing every time.

She let her gaze search his face for signs of pain and when she saw none sighed. "Good. Good."

He grinned and held her gaze for another heartbeat. "Glad you approve."

Gabe grunted and pushed to his feet. "Won't get the job finished sitting in the sun." Gabe had been cleaning up the debris from the roof falling.

But before Gabe could return to the barn, Diana

stepped out. "I just made tea and cookies if anyone is interested."

"I am!" Rachael yelled.

"Then you can help me carry the things outdoors. It's far too nice to be cooped up inside with winter blowing in just about any day."

At the reminder of winter both men looked at the barn.

Virnie understood they were concerned about the fact that one end stood open to the elements.

"I'll be back as soon as we get settled," Gabe said. "Don't you dare touch it until I'm here to help."

"Huh," Conor said and Virnie wondered if he objected to feeling dependent. She knew how he despised any kind of weakness.

It served to warn her how foolish her longings were and she pushed them to the darkest corners of her thoughts. She would never be anything but what she was—a female, sometimes weak, sometimes surprisingly strong, but never quite good enough.

As soon as they finished tea, she got to her feet. "I'll say goodbye." She'd planned to spend the whole afternoon and evening here but knew it was time to stop pretending.

"Aww, why don't you stay?" Rachael said.

"Yes, please do," Diana added.

Gabe nodded. "I know it's not my home but I see no reason for you to rush away."

"You're welcome to stay," Conor said.

But his invitation felt like nothing more than an echo of what the others said. "I need to get back to town and tend to other things." She darted a quick glance at Conor, wondering if she saw regret in his eyes or was it only resignation—acceptance of her responsibilities as a teacher?

"You'll come tomorrow?" His words smoothed away the dark edges of her thoughts, renewing her hope.

"If you'd like."

"Yah!" Rachael cheered, eliminating the need for anyone else to answer but Virnie was certain she caught a flash of pleasure in Conor's eyes.

Somehow, even though she suspected how this would end—with Conor disappointed with her and her heart filled with failure—she couldn't put her hopes and longings to rest. Not yet.

Saturday morning, she forced herself to do her laundry and leave it on a line in her bedroom to dry. She corrected the children's papers and began another letter to Miss Price. But by lunch she couldn't make herself wait another minute and left the letter to finish another day.

"I'm off to check on Rachael at the farm," she called to Mrs. Maxwell, still using that excuse to convince herself her visit was strictly professional. She wondered if anyone still believed it.

At the farm, she discovered Rachael had already baked cookies. "They smell delicious. My mouth has been watering for the last mile from the delicious smell."

Rachael beamed. "You can have one if you want."

"Thank you." She made a show about choosing the nicest-looking one and bit into it. "Umm. As good as it looks." She chewed two more bites. "Where's your pa?"

Diana answered. "He and Gabe are looking at the barn and making plans."

Just then the men stomped in. Conor still limped badly.

"We could smell those cookies." Gabe tickled Rachael and made her laugh. "Enough to make a man forget his work." He took a handful and stepped back to let Conor do the same.

Conor smiled at Virnie. She ducked, feeling as if he sent silent messages that she didn't want the others to see. "Good cookies, Rae. I hope you wrote the recipe down so you can do this again."

"I did, Pa."

"See ya later." Gabe wandered outside.

Conor sat at the table and ate his cookies, a thoughtful look on his face.

Aware of his meditative silence, Virnie kept a guarded eye on him as she helped Diana clean the kitchen and begin supper preparations.

An hour later Gabe returned to the house. "Well, that's done."

Diana chuckled. "And what would that be?"

"I've finished cleaning up the mess Conor made bringing down the roof. I tacked a piece of canvas over the end of the barn. It will serve to keep out any nasty weather. Tomorrow, you and I, Mrs. Winston, are going home." He grabbed her and danced her around the room, making her laugh.

"I can hardly wait to see my house," Diana said when he finally released her.

"You've wasted enough time here." Conor sounded weary.

Gabe punched him lightly on the shoulder. "Don't recall wasting a minute of it."

"No, you've worked hard. I owe you."

"And I'm expecting repayment in two ways."

Conor studied his friend with narrowed eyes. "Yeah?"

"Yup. When I'm ready to put my new barn up you can come and help."

"And the second?"

Gabe's grin flattened and he gave Conor a hard look. "I want you to promise you won't try to rebuild your barn until I return to help you."

The men studied each other. Virnie held her breath. She knew if Conor promised he would keep his promise and they could all stop worrying he'd be hurt again. But she knew how hard it was for him to accept limitations. He saw them as weaknesses and something he could not tolerate in either himself or others.

She knew, like she'd known since she was a child, that she could not live up to such a standard.

Suddenly Conor laughed, a great barking laugh that made them all jump. "I have no intention of getting myself pinned under a beam again. You can count on that."

"Shake?" Gabe held out his hand.

Conor grabbed it and they shook firmly.

Virnie was grateful for the nearby cupboard as relief left her knees shaking. She leaned against it and waited for the feeling to pass.

Gabe grabbed Diana about the waist. "How about you and I go for a walk? I haven't even had time to show you all the beauties of this farm."

From the way they looked at each other, Virnie guessed they wouldn't look farther than the person beside them.

Rachael chased Tippy outside.

Virnie and Conor were alone in the house. Alone for the first time since his accident. Suddenly Virnie felt as uncomfortable as if he were a stranger.

"I'd ask you to go for a walk, too, but I think the best I can do is invite you to sit on the bench outside the door and enjoy the sunshine with me."

He rose and held out his hand.

Her nerves so jumpy she could barely walk, she took his hand and followed him outside where she pulled away and folded her palms together in a lady-like fashion.

They sat side by side looking at the barn and corrals. If she shifted to the right, she could see down the road. If she shifted her gaze to the left—

She'd see Conor so she stared straight ahead.

"The sun feels good," he said.

She didn't want to talk about the sun, the weather or the farm. She wanted to talk about them but didn't know how to start. "You and Rachael have been through so much. She seems to be healed up. I guess it will take some time for your leg to be well again."

"Yet I feel stronger than I ever have."

Virnie jolted with surprise. "How can that be?"

"Because I've discovered…" He paused.

Slowly she brought her gaze to his, saw something warm and reassuring.

"I discovered needing help isn't a weakness."

"Weakness. You could never accept that, could you?" It made her feel unvalued and unacceptable. "Like my pa."

"Your father was wrong in making you feel inadequate. You've proved you aren't." His look went on and on, searching her heart.

She shook her head. "Like Miss Price said, 'Better to dwell on your strengths.'"

"Strange." He captured her hand. "I would have agreed not so long ago."

His touch filled her with confusion. His words seemed to hint at something she could trust. "And now?"

"Now it seems to me that admitting my weaknesses or my need doesn't make me helpless but victorious."

She swallowed hard, her thoughts a tangled mess of wanting, fear and—she didn't know what. "I don't understand."

He traced little circles on the back on her hand. "Weakness and need is not the same as fear or giving up."

She tried to imagine what he meant. "I have weaknesses."

"And strengths."

"Like shaping young minds." It was the one thing she'd been taught she was good at.

"And not-so-young minds."

She couldn't look away from his forceful gaze. Did he mean what she wanted him to mean? Or was he only revealing gratitude again? He'd mentioned fear. And fear gripped her heart, squeezing it dry of every other emotion. Once she'd wanted approval so much she hated herself for not getting it. It had taken a long time to get over that.

She would never go back to that dark, lonesome, lonely place.

He must have read her withdrawal even though she didn't move a muscle. "Virnie, you are a very strong woman. Not just a good teacher but so much more."

She stood and walked away two steps before she turned to face him. "You only see me as what you want me to be." Before he could reply, she ducked into the house, intent on finding a task but Diana had left her nothing to do.

Conor lounged in the doorway. "You don't have to run from me. You don't have to be afraid of me. I am not your father."

She flung around to face him. "What's that supposed to mean."

He shrugged one shoulder. "He said and did things to hurt you. I can't say why but my guess is he was a hurting man. Perhaps afraid of his own weaknesses just like I was until recently."

"No doubt you were scared as you lay pinned under that pile of dirt." She couldn't stop a shudder from rippling across her shoulders. Didn't care that he saw her reaction and his eyes narrowed, as if reading more into it than he had a right. "Once your leg is all better you'll forget this big change in your thoughts. You'll be back to despising any weaknesses. And I've already admitted I have weaknesses." Right now her insides felt like liquid butter. So weak she could barely breathe.

"I don't care. I have weaknesses, too. Together we balance each other. Together we are strong."

She wanted to believe he had changed. She

wanted to believe he could accept her weaknesses but she couldn't. She didn't dare. "Someday you would grow to hate my weaknesses."

"No, Virnie, I promise I wouldn't." He took a step toward her.

His blue eyes blazed, signaling his intention.

She loved him. Wanted him to love her but it frightened her to her very core with its expectations. She held out a hand and backed away.

He stopped. The flame in his eyes died.

She hated to see his hurt but she couldn't help it. She couldn't get past her fear even though she wanted to.

Lord, God, help me forget my past and be able to face whatever the future might hold.

She shivered with anticipation at the idea of a future shared with a loving man. But her fear reared its head and her shivers turned to a shudder.

Conor turned and hobbled outside. He stood in the middle of the yard feeling more helpless than at any time in his life. Why couldn't he persuade Virnie to trust him?

Trust wasn't easy. He knew that from experience. Look at how he'd struggled against trusting God when it was the very thing he needed.

He limped to the corral fence and leaned over the top rail. *God, she's been hurt far more than she realizes. But You reached me with Your healing and*

I know You can reach her, too. Please do so. I love her and I want to share my life with her.

He thought of returning to the house and declaring his love in loud, clear terms but somehow he understood she wasn't ready to hear the words. Until she was, he would be patient and try not to push her.

Rae raced up to him. "Virnie's leaving. Tell her to stay."

He turned.

Virnie faced him across the yard. "I think it best if I go back to town."

"There isn't any point in arguing, is there?"

She shook her head.

"Hadn't you better wait for Gabe and Diana to return so you can say goodbye to them?"

She glanced along the path the pair had taken. They were almost back.

He sighed. If he'd hoped that would provide a reason for her to stay... he'd have to find another even though he knew she would have to find the reason in her own heart.

Rae ran to meet Gabe and Diana.

Conor closed the distance between him and Virnie. "I don't want you to leave like this." He couldn't stop himself from stroking her cheek, reveling in the silky softness of her skin. He glowed inwardly when she didn't jerk away. "You could stay for supper. After all, it's Gabe and Diana's last day here."

She ducked her eyes then slowly lifted them to his. "I wish I could feel differently. Maybe in time…"

He laughed. "Virnie White, in case you didn't notice there's nothing much but time out here on the prairie. I'll be here waiting until you're ready."

She nodded. "No promises."

"Except mine to wait."

It was all he could do not to drape his arm across her shoulder as they joined Gabe and Diana at the house.

Sunday morning, Gabe and Diana left shortly after daybreak. "Got to get home before dark," Gabe said.

"Thank you for everything. And in case I didn't say it, congratulations to you both on your marriage."

Rae hugged them both then ran after her kitten.

Gabe leaned over and whispered loudly. "I hope you corral Virnie before someone else does."

"I'm doing my best."

Gabe laughed uproariously at that.

They drove away, looking back often to wave goodbye.

Conor waited until they were out of sight to return to the house. Suddenly it felt very empty. He was more alone than he had ever been. He'd promised to give Virnie all the time she needed. He hoped that wouldn't be long. He was not a patient man.

"Rae, are you ready for church?"

She dashed in. "Just let me change."

He waited for her to put on her dress. Funny how he'd thought wearing a dress would make her weak. She could put on a dress for church and just as easily put on overalls when she got home. She still milked the cow faster than any man. And she managed the household chores much better thanks to both Virnie and Diana.

When they rode to church, they found Virnie waiting at the steps for them. His heart leaped with joy. At least she wasn't pushing him out of her life. They entered the church together and sat side by side in a pew, Rae at Virnie's other side. This was the way he wanted his life to be. Sharing daily events, sharing faith, sharing work and dreams. It was all he could do not to reach for Virnie's hand as they sat together especially when she flashed him a smile so full of warmth and promise that his lungs forgot to work.

He forced himself to concentrate on the sermon and was glad he didn't miss a word of the pastor's encouragement to trust God through both the good and bad things of life.

When the service ended, he didn't want to move. It felt so good and right to sit here with Virnie. He silently prayed the sermon had encouraged her as much as it had him. If she could put her past away and embrace the future…a future shared with him.

"Did Gabe and Diana get away all right?"

He sighed. Her thoughts were obviously not going the direction he hoped. "Left at first light."

"Diana must be anxious to see her new home." Virnie got to her feet and waited for Conor to stand. "Are your legs sore after sitting so long?"

Let her think his hesitation came from pain in his legs not reluctance in his heart. But he didn't want to cause her undue worry. "No worse than any other time." He pushed to his feet, stood a moment without moving as his tender feet adjusted to his weight.

Several people stopped them as they headed down the aisle. "Heard about your accident. Glad to see you in one piece." "Good to see you walking about." "Be sure and let us know if you need help. Anytime."

They reached the door. Conor wanted to stop time right there before they had to part ways. He thought of inviting her out for the afternoon. Not appropriate. Maybe he could spend the day in town.

Mrs. Brown, whose husband ran the general store, stepped aside as they passed and turned to the woman next to her. "I hear our little schoolteacher spends a great deal of time out at the Russell farm."

Conor gave the woman a hard look. He knew her words had been intended for everyone to hear. The woman returned him hard look for hard look, clearly informing him as well as all those watching what she thought about the situation.

Rae, wanting to defend her beloved teacher, announced loudly, "Miss White comes out all the time. She's teaching me to cook and clean. Isn't that right, Pa?"

Conor groaned. He'd taught Rae to be fearless. But he hadn't counted on having it backfire. He stole a look at Virnie. The color had drained from her face. Her eyes were wide with shock.

He heard several tsks from various directions.

Mr. Nelson, a school board member, marched over to face Virnie. "What's this I hear? Is it true? Are you spending time at a farm without adequate chaperoning?" His voice condemned both Conor and Virnie.

Conor stepped forward. "Now wait a minute. What you suggest is totally unfounded. Miss White has been teaching Rae—" He struggled for a word. "Domestic science. Very commendable that she would go beyond classroom expectations."

"Humph." Mrs. Brown's disapproval was evident.

"And my friend Gabe Winston and his wife,

Diana, have been there. They only left this morning."

Mr. Nelson shook his finger at Virnie. "Miss White, you have a responsibility to maintain a flawless reputation and to devote yourself to all the children, not just one."

Conor wanted to grab the offending member of the man's hand and shove it down his throat.

Virnie nodded. "You are correct. Now if you'll all excuse me…" She swept down the road toward the Maxwell house.

Conor wondered how she managed to keep her head so high and her stride so unhurried. His heart ached for her. It seemed everyone had high expectations of her, from her father to the school board— though he knew she had reason to watch her conduct before the board. *Lord, help us live wisely.*

He vowed he would find a way to prove to her he accepted her just as she was. More than that, he loved the way she was right now—her fear of spiders, her determination, her noble ideals, her past pain that gave her a vulnerable core he wished he could love to wholeness. *God, am I wanting to do something only You can do? If so, I trust You to do Your work.*

"Come on, Rae. Let's go home."

Rae waited until they rode toward home to ask, "Is Miss White in trouble?"

"I don't think so. After all she hasn't done anything wrong."

"Those people weren't very nice to her."

"Perhaps they didn't mean to be unkind." He couldn't speak for anyone's motivation but wanted no reason for Rae to be upset.

If only he could visit Virnie and reassure her. If only he could tell her he loved her. But he must respect her reservations and give her time to work through their changing feelings for each other.

Chapter Twelve

Virnie kept her head high and her steps measured until she reached the sanctuary of the Maxwell house, then she sped to her bedroom and closed the door. She paced to the window and looked out. What had she done? Nothing. Her conscience was clear. But had she given people cause to wonder otherwise?

She couldn't honestly answer the question. She felt as if she rode a giant rocking horse, tossed from one side to the other by her emotions. First, hope that Conor accepted her, perhaps cared for her deeply, then fear of needing his acceptance. Back to hope for a shared life and a home of her own, then condemnation of her faltering ways.

Lord, show me what You want. Guide me.

She went to school Monday resolved to step back from her feelings toward Conor and not let them control her. Yet she couldn't keep from watching down the road. When Rachael ran to the school on her own, Virnie smiled and pretended she wasn't disappointed Conor hadn't accompanied her.

"Pa said to tell you he had a cow to tend to."

Virnie nodded. "Of course."

She worked hard all day making sure she showed each child the care and attention they needed. She would give no one cause to criticize her.

But part of her heart yearned for things outside the classroom. She loved Conor. And loving made her feel unsettled. As if she'd lost her center of balance. In the past, love had left her needy and unsatisfied. Only devotion to a task, a duty, had made her feel she walked on solid footing. But was it enough? Enough to satisfy for the rest of her life?

She didn't have the answers and didn't know where to find them. *God, You alone have the answers. Show me what is right.*

School ended and she returned to her room. Mrs. Maxwell had left Virnie's mail on the hall table outside her door. Virnie picked up the letter from Miss Price and retreated to her room to read it.

She skimmed the usual greeting and Miss Price's report on the progress of her students. She had another child living with her—Donna—and Miss Price reported the girl showed great promise and dedication.

Virnie gasped at the next paragraph.

You consider that helping a man free himself
from his own folly makes you useful? What
are you thinking? I would suggest you'd be far
more useful if you were to attend to the needs
of all your students. Devoting your time and
energy to one child and her father is to neglect
your duties as a teacher. It is to fail in what
I've striven hard to teach you. It is to nullify
your calling. It is a waste.

Virnie let the pages fall to her lap and stared out
the window. She'd disappointed Miss Price. Let her
down. After all Miss Price had done for her.

She picked up the pages and reread the stern
warning. Here then was her answer. She had set
her heart and mind on being a teacher since the first
day Miss Price had taken her in. She would keep
her course steadily in that direction. She folded the
letter, returned it to the envelope and dropped it in
the drawer along with the other letters from Miss
Price.

She pulled out the lesson plans for the next day
and concentrated on them. This was who she was.
A teacher.

Again the next day, Rachael walked to school on
her own. Virnie was glad. She didn't think she was
up to seeing Conor. Her determination wavered even
at the thought.

Wednesday morning, Conor brought Rachael

on horseback. When she saw them approaching, Virnie hurried into the school. She could not speak to him and successfully quench the yearnings of her heart.

She struggled through the rest of the day, knowing she must focus on her job of teaching yet feeling as if something dear and precious that she hadn't even known existed had been ripped from her.

She bid the children goodbye at the end of the day and remained at her desk. She'd plan the lessons for the next day and start to prepare recitations for the Christmas concert in a month's time.

Suddenly, the door was flung back and Conor stomped to the front of the room, still limping on his right leg.

"Why are you avoiding me?"

She blinked before his fury. "I've been attending to my duties."

"You did so before but that didn't prevent you from sparing me a 'Hello, how are you?'"

She pursed her lips. He was making this far more difficult than it had to be. "Hello. How are you? See you're walking better."

He planted his hands on the edge of the desk and leaned forward. "You can't shut me out. I promised to be patient but I don't plan to walk away."

It hurt her neck to tip her head to meet his gaze, and the intensity in those blue eye sent shards of confusion through her thoughts, messing up her neat and orderly plans. She ducked her head and stared at his big, work-worn hands. Hands that could be gentle and comforting. "I can't be what everyone wants me to be. I can't be a good teacher unless I devote myself to it fully."

"Like Miss Price?"

She jerked her head up in surprise at his words. "Yes, like Miss Price. I owe her so much."

"Who else are you trying to please?"

"What do you mean?"

"You said you couldn't be what everyone wants. Who else do you mean? Your father?"

"I could never be what he wants. He wanted a son."

"Who else?" he demanded in low, insistent tones.

She straightened the papers on her desk and adjusted the ink well.

"Virnie, who else are you trying to please?"

His prodding pushed her to speak without thinking. "I can't be what you want, either. I'm not strong. I'm not pioneer stock."

He leaned back and laughed. When he sobered he crossed his arms over his chest and grinned at her. "Virnie, you hide behind your pretty little ways but both you and I know you can be as tough as you want to be or need to be when the occasion arises."

His look, full of admiration, burned away all her arguments.

She had to explain. Make him see what she must do. "I had a letter from Miss Price reminding me of my decision to be a teacher the rest of my life."

Conor sobered. "Your decision or hers?"

"I don't know what you mean."

He sat on the top of the nearest desk so he could face her. She tried to break their look but his gaze demanded her attention.

"Virnie, perhaps it's time to be who you are. Not what your father appears to have wanted—a boy and seeing as he was stuck with a girl, a girl who passed as a boy. Not what Miss Price wants, someone to be just like her. I don't think either of those is the real you."

Confusion washed through her, leaving her weepy and uncertain. "Then who am I?"

His smile was gentle as morning dew. "I think you know but are afraid to admit it."

She ducked her head and sniffed. "You aren't making any sense."

He slipped from the desk and moved close. He caught her chin and tipped her face toward him.

The look of love in his eyes filled her with such sweet befuddlement. She knew it was a precarious state of mind. For a moment she didn't care then her fear at being needy turned the sweet feeling bitter.

She lowered her eyes even though he still held her chin and settled her gaze on his chest.

"Virnie, it's time you made peace with your past."

She jerked her startled gaze to his. Peace with her past? "It's not possible. How can I accept how I was treated as a child?"

He stroked her chin, his eyes full of longing. "I think you have to accept it. But you've lost contact with both your father and your brother. Doesn't that make you the least bit sad?"

Her heart clenched like someone bound it in cruel ropes. Tears welled up and overspilled. She clenched her teeth to stop from sobbing.

"Ahh. I see it does." He wiped each cheek, capturing the tears with his fingertips. "Have you ever tried to get hold of them?"

She shook her head. "Miss Price—" She couldn't finish.

"Miss Price forbade it?"

"Said it wasn't wise."

His look probed deep into her soul, exposing unhealed wounds, hungry longings, regrets she couldn't confess. "Virnie, what do you want?"

"I want to see Miles again. He was a good brother to me. He took me with him everywhere he went and tended me like a mother. In fact, he was both mother and father to me." The enormity of her loss choked her words.

Conor stroked her hair. "Seems to me you are mourning him when he's likely still alive and well. Why not see if you can find him?"

She struggled with her longing. So many years she'd denied it. Pretended nothing mattered except being like Miss Price. Pleasing her. Yet she couldn't forget Miles. "I remember crying for him after I went to live with Miss Price until she finally said I must forget him and everything about my past."

"I think you almost succeeded but perhaps there has always been an ache that wouldn't go away."

She stared at him through her tears. "How do you know all this?"

He chuckled. "Wasn't too many days ago I was trying so hard to forget my own past or maybe push it into a different shape, one that didn't fit." He smiled softly, making her feel trembly inside. "I discovered I can't push the past away but I must learn from it and build on it."

Her ache to see Miles slowly filled her to the point she couldn't imagine why she hadn't tried to find him long ago. "What if he doesn't want to see me?"

"I'll pray he does. And even if he doesn't, at least you will have done what you can."

She bolted to her feet. "I'm going to send a letter tonight." Before her well-developed denial process sprang back into control. She hesitated as she came face-to-face with him. "I hope I'm not setting myself up for major heartache."

"Are you getting ready to blame me?"

She shook her head, then changed her mind and nodded. Then she stopped altogether. "I'll let you know when I hear back—if I hear back. Who knows if I'll even be able to contact him?"

He squeezed her shoulder. "I'll pray."

"Thank you." His touch settled her and she turned back to gather her lessons.

He walked her to the door. Rachael waited by the horse. "I'll say goodbye here rather than give Mrs. Brown any reason for more gossip."

She said goodbye to both Conor and Rachael and hurried home. But when she sat down to pen the letter, she couldn't think what to say. Remembering how Conor promised to pray, she bowed her head and asked for wisdom, then picked up the pen and wrote a simple letter saying she had never forgotten him and would like to see him if he was agreeable.

She addressed the envelope to the town nearest the Zingle farm where she had spent many hours helping Miles. She had no idea if he still lived in the same area but if not she hoped the postmaster would know where to forward the letter.

She took the letter to the post office immediately before she could change her mind.

That night she lay in bed, unable to sleep. She

would love to see Miles again. But for what purpose? By morning she regretted her impulsive decision. If she could she would retrieve the letter but it was already on its way.

This was Conor's fault. He was all fired up because he'd made some wonderful discoveries while praying for rescue. Virnie didn't think she needed to risk death to know what she was or what she needed. She did not need approval of her father, her brother or Conor. Seeking it in the past had left her with nothing but aching wounds that Conor's probing had uncovered, renewing the pain and uncertainty they carried.

When he rode to the school with Rachael, Virnie had a fine level of annoyance built and spared him a long, accusing look before she turned away.

After school, she waited at the gate, her arms full of papers and books when Conor arrived. As soon as he was close enough that she could safely leave Rachael, she headed for home without so much as a backward look. At least she didn't need to worry about Rachael. She had no lingering doubts that Conor loved his daughter. And Virnie herself had taught the child enough skills to ensure they would eat some decent meals and eat off clean dishes.

She had been perfectly content with her life until he poked his nose into her business.

Nevertheless, she hurried to the hall table to check for mail. There was none.

Every day for the next week, she checked for a letter from Miles.

There was none and she grew more despondent and blamed Conor. She would have never written that letter, awakened that hope, without his prodding.

She had tried to avoid him at church. No need to give the good ladies of the area any reason to criticize her. But two weeks later, he waited after church until she had no choice but to head for home. He fell into step beside her, leading Noble, with Rachael racing ahead.

Virnie tried to convince herself she didn't care that it obviously still hurt him to walk.

"I take it you haven't heard from Miles."

She sniffed. "I should have never listened to you."

"I never made you do anything. I thought it was what you wanted to do."

The fact that his words rang with truth didn't make them any easier to swallow. "Strange, don't you think, that in the past seven years I've never considered writing him? Not until now."

"Now that you mention it, yes." Only his tone was a lot more accusing than regretful.

She flung him a glance full of fury. "Sometimes a person learns to accept things and not wish they could be different."

He slowed so he could look into her face as he

talked. "What things do you wish you could change, Virnie?"

"Nothing. That's just the point. I've accepted my life the way it is."

"Accepted?"

"Don't scoff."

"Accepted sounds like trying to scrape up the dregs and convince yourself it's better than the best. Why would you settle for that?"

His words drove through her heart, pinpointing what she tried so hard to hide. "Because it hurts too much to wish for things that can't be." She stomped away, as angry at herself for confessing her fear as at him for pushing her past her endurance.

"Maybe they can be."

"What?" The man talked in more riddles than a clown.

"Maybe the things you want can happen."

She stormed on without speaking.

He kept pace even though his feet must be hurting something awful by now. Or, maybe they didn't. Maybe they were better. She didn't know, having avoided talking to him for two weeks.

He caught her elbow.

She didn't slow down.

"Virnie, what is it you want? Love, belonging, acceptance? I can give you those if you let me. I love—"

She couldn't bear to hear it. "No one can give

me what I want." The enormity of the words she'd uttered made her stumble.

Conor caught her. "Careful there."

No one could give her what she wanted because… the truth hit her like a blast of hot wind straight off the prairie…because she wouldn't let them.

Thankfully they had reached the Maxwell home. "Good day." She rushed inside, her thoughts driving her straight to her room where she closed the door and leaned against it, panting as if she had run a thousand yards.

She wouldn't let them.

The words circled around her like vultures.

Why wouldn't she let them?

It didn't make sense. She fell to her knees at the side of the bed. *Lord, God, help me. I am lost and can't find my way. Be Thou my guide.*

The days passed. Christmas slowly approached. It should be a time of joy and anticipation. For Virnie it was not.

Miles had not written. She'd given up hope he would.

She refused to see Conor other than to nod curtly when they met in church or when he gave Rachael a ride to and from school. Her only excuse was to blame him for triggering her hope that things could be different.

She tried to balance the attention she gave

Rachael with what the others needed. Yet her heart called her back to Rachael time after time. The child watched her with brown-eyed sadness.

"You don't like me anymore, do you?" Rachael's question tore raw strips from Virnie's heart.

"Oh, sweetie, I love you." She knew she should not say the words to a student, but she also understood Rachael did not need to carry any idea of rejection with her.

"Then why don't you come visit anymore?"

"It's something grown-ups have to work out, but it's not because of you. Never think that."

Rachael ducked her head but not before Virnie saw the pain and retreat. She regressed into being a tough little tomboy.

Virnie wished she could push her thoughts and emotions back to where they had been when she first came to Sterling but, no thanks to Conor, they proved impossible to control.

One question dogged her every waking hour and filled her nights with restless torment.

Why wouldn't she let people give her what she wanted? She could say what she wanted, had known it since she was very young. She wanted acceptance, approval, love—probably all part of the same thing.

Conor had offered them to her.

She couldn't accept.

And she couldn't explain why it was so.

As was expected of her, she prepared Christmas surprises for the children, filling each little sack with a handful of candies and an orange.

The night of the concert was cold and clear. Snow from a few days ago covered the brown-and-yellow landscape of fall with fresh white.

The men had arrived after class to push the desks together and set up benches along the edges. Mr. Nelson had hung up bedsheets earlier in the week to serve as a curtain for the stage. Everything was ready. Each of the children had a speaking part and they had rehearsed several songs.

"Come on, children." They had gathered behind the curtain and she clapped for their attention. "You all look very nice." The boys wore their best white shirts. All the girls had on their best dresses. Rachael wore a brand-new dress.

"Pa bought it for me," she whispered to Virnie.

"It's lovely," she whispered back and gave the girl a quick hug before she turned her attention to the rest of the students. "Now remember what I said. Smile. And do your best."

The children nodded, anxious to please her and do a good job. She let satisfaction smooth away her silly notions about belonging and accepting love. This was where she belonged. With children. Teaching them, shaping them, molding them and preparing them to be the best they could be.

It felt much safer than dealing with her inner turmoil.

Enough of such nonsense. She pushed her confusion to the back recesses of her mind, stepped to the center of the stage, parted the curtain and faced the audience. The room was crowded with parents and neighbors. Conor sat dead front. She carefully avoided looking at him.

He could offer her what she wanted.

She wouldn't let him give it to her.

Why?

She again forced her thoughts into submission and welcomed everyone.

The children did a good job. The two Schmidt boys spoke flawless English as they recited a poem she had written especially for them.

Hilda and her little sisters, Gracie and Alice, sang a Christmas song.

George recited the entire second chapter of Luke.

She hugged each and every one of them when the concert was finished. "You did a wonderful job." Yes, this was where she belonged. She felt safe with children. Besides, good teachers were needed. Always would be.

The candy bags were handed to the children and the adults rose to visit with friends and neighbors. Conor moved to the back as if he didn't want to endure Virnie's continued avoidance of him. She barely noticed as each parent made a point of speaking to her, thanking her for the good job she had done and wishing her a blessed Christmas. School would be closed now for two weeks that stretched before her as endless as winter.

She stole a forbidden glance in Conor's direction. He spoke to a man who stood with his back to Virnie. If only Conor's back was to her so she couldn't see that face, those eyes.

Slowly, as if reluctant to end the evening, people drifted away. Conor hung about. She wondered if he wanted to speak to her and busied herself with putting away decorations. She couldn't face him, more correctly couldn't face the quagmire of her inner turmoil.

"Virnie."

She turned. A man faced her. Not someone from the community. Her heart stalled. Her thoughts froze. "Miles?"

The man nodded. "It's me."

Out of the corner of her eye, she saw Conor take Rachael's hand and slip away.

"Miles." Her voice choked off. She couldn't move. Couldn't breathe. Couldn't think.

Chapter Thirteen

"Who was that, Pa?" Rae asked as he tucked her into the buggy he'd recently pulled from the corner of the barn and cleaned up. It had sat unused long enough…since Irene's death.

"That was Miss White's brother."

"The one she hasn't seen in a long time?"

"Yup."

"I hope it makes her happy again."

"Me, too." He'd tried to explain to Rae that Virnie's retreat from them was because she was unhappy. "I think he'll help her find what she needs." He prayed it would.

He'd had a chance to speak to Miles. He liked the man. Straightforward and outgoing. He seemed eager to see Virnie. Conor smiled. That might have been his reason for liking Miles. Anyone who revealed that much affection for Virnie earned approval in Conor's eyes.

The last few weeks had been difficult. Loving Virnie yet being forced to stand back and wait for her to come to terms with who she was. It stretched his rediscovered faith. But one thing he knew— he wasn't about to give up. She'd find in him the strength and staying power she needed.

He prayed God would provide whatever else she needed.

"I invited her brother to join us for Christmas," he told Rae.

"And bring Virnie, too?"

"That was the idea."

Rae giggled. "Won't she be surprised when she sees how big Tippy is and opens the present we bought her?"

"I 'spect so." He'd forced himself to buy her only a small present though he wanted to buy every nice trinket in the store.

Rae squirmed in excitement. "With Uncle Gabe and Auntie Diana coming, too, it will make six of us. It's going to be the best Christmas ever."

Conor hoped she wasn't getting her hopes up for nothing. "We don't know for sure Virnie and her brother will come."

In the moonlight glistening off the snow he watched Rae lift her face to the sky, her eyes squeezed tight.

"What are you doing?"

"Praying they come." She blinked and turned wide-eyed to him. "That's all right, isn't it?"

"I should think so, though we have to be prepared God might not choose to force her. We want her to come because she wants to."

Virnie took a faltering step toward Miles and halted.

He held out his arms. "Virnie, my baby sister."

She ran into his arms, clutching his lapels as tears streamed down her face. "I didn't think you would come," she managed to say.

"I came as soon as I got your letter." He hugged her tight.

If she wasn't mistaken he sounded as choked as she.

"The letter caught up with me west of here. I've been thinking of starting a ranch."

She leaned back and studied his face. He was heavier than she remembered, fuller in the face. Yet his eyes were the same soft brown she recalled. He wore better clothes than they had as children. A rough woolen coat with a white shirt beneath. She remembered him once holding her close as she cried, the reason now forgotten but the feel of his arms about her felt the same. Solid. Comforting. Even though her chin now rested on his shoulder rather than his chest. "You're older."

He chuckled, a familiar sound that made

her smile. "You are, too. But my, you look like Mama."

She scrubbed her lips together a minute before she could talk. "I don't remember Mama at all."

"Don't you remember how she used to pull you to her lap and tell you to always be strong? I think she knew she wouldn't live to raise you."

Virnie shook her head. "I don't remember."

Miles laughed again. "You would always pop down to stand in front of her and flex your arm like you'd seen me do. 'I very strong,' you'd say and we'd all laugh."

Brother and sister stared at each other.

Miles pulled her close again. "My little sister, how I've missed you."

She sobbed against his shoulder as she thought of all the years they had lost. He held her, patting her back as she cried out her sorrow. Tears were supposed to heal or so she'd heard, but she didn't find they did. Her insides felt raw, oozing pain she couldn't control. All she could do was push it back into the cages she had built for it.

She sniffed away the last of her tears and straightened, wiping at Miles's coat where she'd soaked it. "Sorry. I didn't expect to be so emotional."

He chuckled, the sound rattling the bars of her cages. "Me neither."

She laughed to see his face tear-streaked, too.

He pulled out a big hanky and wiped her face and then dried his own.

"Do you have a place to spend the night?"

"I'm staying in a room behind the general store."

Virnie knew of the place the Browns let to travelers. "It's adequate."

"I've slept in far worse."

Together they circled the schoolroom, turning out the lamps and making sure everything was secure.

"How long are you staying?" she asked.

"Anxious to get rid of me already?"

She recognized the teasing in his voice and remembered how he had teased her as a child and made her laugh. She laughed now. "I'm afraid you'll go and leave me alone again."

He grabbed her shoulders. "Virnie, now that I've found you I don't intend to let you out of my sight for a long time. In fact, I thought I might hang around here until spring."

Virnie couldn't stop smiling. "I'm glad." She'd been dreading the holidays without school to occupy her but now she couldn't wait to spend every day learning about Miles and what happened to him since they last saw each other. She had to know one more thing before they stepped out into the cold. "Papa?"

"I'm sorry. He died about a year ago."

She cried out with pain.

He held her.

"I didn't expect it to matter." But how would she ever resolve the need to prove herself to him? "Let's go." She pulled the door closed behind them.

They said good-night outside the Maxwell house and arranged to meet right after breakfast the next morning.

As Virnie prepared for bed, she laughed softly with joy that Miles had come. But her joy dissolved into hot tears. How could she ever let Conor give her what she wanted when it was now impossible to get it from her father? She wept into her pillow. She couldn't even say what she cried over—loss of a father who had sent her away, the death of hope for a chance to share her life with Conor?

The next two days spent with Miles were sweet delight to her starving soul—something she had been unaware of until she started to feed it with memories and shared affection of her brother.

"Conor invited us to spend Christmas Day with him," Miles said.

Virnie had told him about the days spent helping Rachael and how she'd rescued Conor.

Miles had laughed long and hard at that. "Just like you were at Mama's knees. 'I strong.'"

She hadn't confessed her love for Conor. She'd avoided spending time with him afraid of her own needy longing. But she wanted him to get to know Miles. "I'd like that."

"Then I need to buy some gifts."

"Me, too." She had already bought a nice fur muff for Rachael but had avoided thinking of a gift for Conor.

With Miles at her side, she enjoyed shopping. In the end they selected gifts for all who'd be at the farm, including Gabe and Diana.

Her anticipation of spending the day in Conor's company seemed to grow with every gift they bought, every story she and Miles shared and every heartbeat that marked the time until they went to the farm. She loved him. Knew he loved her. She yearned to be able to embrace that love. But a fearful lump tailed after her anticipation.

It wasn't until she was alone in her room that her fear made its full fury known. She sat on the edge of her bed shivering. What was she so afraid of that she couldn't accept love?

Lord, there is something dreadfully wrong with me. I don't know what it is or how to correct it. Surely You do. A verse sprang to mind. *"My substance was not hid from Thee, when I was made in secret." Lord, You made me. You know how to fix me. Please do Your work.*

Christmas day dawned cold and clear.

Rachael had been up long before the sun, staring

at the gifts under the tree. Conor wondered what he'd do for a Christmas tree but Gabe brought one with him.

"Pa, how long do we have to wait?"

"Until I do the chores and we eat breakfast." He hoped if he delayed long enough, Virnie and her brother would show up.

"Aww."

Diana was busy at the stove. Gabe drank coffee. Conor grabbed the milk bucket. He took care of that task now that it was cold. No need for Rae to do it when he had to go to the barn anyway. "I'll do chores and then return to eat."

He prayed as he milked the cow then forked up feed for the animals. *Lord, it's hard to be patient when I want so badly to share my love and my life with Virnie. But I will trust You. I will allow You to heal her and set her free to love.*

He vowed he would do his best to make the day one to remember even if Virnie didn't choose to join them.

He returned to the house, pausing to look down the road. He saw nothing. Told himself he didn't expect to. Inside, he took care of the milk then sat down at the table. He had just finished blessing the food when he heard the thud of horse hooves and the rattle and creak of a conveyance.

It was all he could do not to bolt for the window like Rae did.

"It's Virnie and her brother," she announced.

The room brightened like the sun had suddenly come from behind a cloud.

"I'll set two more places," Diana said.

Conor grabbed his coat and went out to help put the horse in the barn. He reached the side of the buggy almost before Miles drew to a halt and reached up to assist Virnie. "Glad you could make it," he murmured, shaking hands with Miles and then helping her to alight, holding her several moments more than necessary.

She met his gaze and smiled. He saw in her look a sweetness, an assurance perhaps even a happiness he had not seen before.

"It's been good for you to see your brother."

She tipped her head and pretended to grow serious. "Indeed. And how would you know that?"

He chuckled. "See it in your eyes."

She ducked away and reached back to gather a handful of packages. "I think you see far too much. Here, take these."

He helped her with the parcels. "I think I see far too little."

She stilled and slowly faced him, all teasing gone from her expression. "I'm rediscovering my love for my brother."

Her words effectively informed him it was nothing more. "It's a start." And as such gave him renewed hope for more. He led them indoors.

Rae rushed forward to greet them, hesitated. Virnie held out her arms, inviting Rae into a hug, then she turned toward Miles. "Rachael, this my brother, Miles."

Miles shook hands. "Pleased to meet you. Virnie speaks of you in glowing terms."

Rae beamed.

Conor introduced the others and together they moved toward the table and sat down.

At Rae's urging they hurried through breakfast so they could gather around the tree. There seemed an overabundance of gifts. Conor realized he had neglected this holiday in the past, deprived Rae of so much pleasure and silently, he thanked these dear friends for showing him the need for change.

He handed Virnie the gift he and Rae had chosen together.

She gave him a warm smile that seemed full of promise before she folded back the paper to reveal the stack of pretty writing paper with matching envelopes, all tied with a bright pink ribbon. "It's lovely. Thank you." She hugged Rae as she glanced at Conor.

He hoped the warmth in her eyes signaled a change in her heart about trusting love.

She had given him a very handsome tie. And laughed at his surprise. "I thought you might like to wear it on Sundays."

He couldn't help wondering and wishing that

perhaps, just for a moment, she had imagined him wearing it at their wedding because that was his first thought when he saw it. It was a wonderful gift. One he would cherish always. "Thank you. It means more to me than you can imagine."

Rae got a fur muff from Virnie, a little doll from Diana and Gabe, and from Miles, a storybook. Conor waited until the end of the gift exchange to bring out his gift for Rae—a child-sized saddle.

"Pa?" He knew her unspoken question. What was she to do with a saddle?

"I think it might be just a perfect fit for the pony in the barn."

Rae bound to her feet and raced for the door, slowing to get her coat only because Conor called after her.

"I've got to see this," Gabe followed.

Conor grabbed the saddle and the rest crowded after like a gaggle of excited children.

In the barn, Rae walked around the black-and-white pony, patting his rump and running her fingers through his mane. "He's perfect."

She darted to Conor and jumped into his arms to hug and kiss him. "Thank you, Pa."

"What are you going to call him?"

She thought for a moment. "Prince. His name is Prince."

"Fine name for a fine horse," Conor said. The others nodded approval.

"Can I ride him?"

"He's yours. I guess you better try him out." He supervised putting on the saddle, pleased to see she could handle it well. He handed her the bridle and made sure she got it in place. When he reached out to help her mount she shook her head.

"I want to do it all by myself."

"Very well." Best if she did. That way she would be safe riding to school and back and wherever she wanted.

It took several attempts before she figured out how to reach the stirrup and pull herself up. But she did it.

And he couldn't have been prouder.

He watched Rae ride up and down the alleyway and then he opened the door and let her ride down the road.

Virnie stood at his side. "You've made her very happy."

"It's practical to have her able to get around on her own."

Virnie laughed. "Yes. I'm sure that was upper-most in your thoughts when you bought her the pony." She nudged him, tipping his heart far more than she tipped his body. "You don't fool any of us. You knew how much she'd enjoy being able to ride."

The others chuckled, too.

"She's got you figured out, old man," Gabe chortled.

He suddenly wished the rest of them would disappear and leave him alone with Virnie so he could tell her what would give him even more pleasure than seeing Rae so happy—her acceptance of his love.

But none of them made a move to go elsewhere.

He let Rae ride around a bit longer than called her back. He made sure she put away the tack and brushed her horse.

"Can I stay with him for a while?"

"Sure."

Gabe pulled Diana close. "We're going for a walk."

"The turkey is in the oven. There's nothing to do for a little while," Diana called over her shoulder as they departed.

"We might as well go inside." Conor hoped the two of them would share something that would give him reason to believe Miles's visit would work a miracle in Virnie's heart.

"Anyone care for tea?" Virnie asked, setting about to prepare it without waiting for an answer.

"How do you like Sterling?" Conor asked Miles.

"Nice little town. Mostly farming around here though, isn't it?"

"Miles is interested in ranching," Virnie said, beaming at her brother.

Conor wanted to grab her gaze and make her look at him the same way. He wanted to hear all about her reunion with her brother.

But by the time she finished fussing with tea, Gabe and Diana returned. "It's cold out there." Diana shivered.

And of course, Virnie had to make more tea and put out more cups and fuss about Diana getting too cold.

Then Rae returned. "I'm hungry."

Diana opened a box of cookies to go with the tea.

All the time, Conor could think of nothing but the questions burning at the back of his mind. How was her visit with Miles going? Had it made a difference for her?

Perhaps the others were as curious for different reasons because Diana turned to Miles. "I understand it's been a while since you last saw Virnie."

"Over seven years." He appeared choked up for a moment. "I wondered if I would ever see her again."

"She was just a child when you last saw her then. You must notice quite a change."

Miles grinned at Virnie. "You wouldn't believe what an adventuresome child she was. She'd tackle anything from a rank cow to trying to lift fork loads of hay as big as I did."

Conor snorted. "She caught my bull in a head-lock. Said you taught her how to do it."

Miles laughed and slapped his knee. "I can just see it."

All eyes turned to Virnie. Although her cheeks stained a very pretty pink she shook her head. "I had to be tough."

Miles snorted. "You seemed to think you did." He turned to the others. "I figured the only way I could keep her from being hurt on the farm was to teach her as much as I could. She was scared of nothing."

"She's scared of spiders," Rae piped up.

Conor laughed. "Not always." Of course he had to then explain how Virnie had rescued him even though the place crawled with spiders.

Diana turned back to Miles. "But why was Virnie with you? You couldn't have been more than a boy. Didn't you have parents?"

"Our mother died," Miles explained.

"And Papa left me alone," Virnie added.

Miles nodded. "She wasn't yet school-age but the summer was upon us and I had a job at a nearby farm so I took her with me. I didn't like thinking of her alone all day."

Virnie shuddered. "I hated it. I didn't know if everyone would go away for good like Mama had.

There were so many things I couldn't do. I couldn't even brush a spider off my hair." She shuddered and gasped. "That's when I developed my fear of them. I remember one crawling into my hair and I couldn't get it out." She shuddered again.

"Yuck," Rae said.

Conor sat next to Virnie and squeezed her hands. "I learned how awful it is to have them crawl around on you and not be able to brush them off."

She sent him a grateful look.

Diana jumped to her feet. "Here I am forgetting about the meal. Christmas dinner. Tsk."

Virnie jolted to her feet to help.

Miles leaned back. "Do you intend to rebuild the barn?"

"Have materials for a wooden one. A real barn."

"That's why I'm here," Gabe said. "I'm going to help him."

"Could you use another set of hands?"

"Of course," Gabe and Conor chorused as one.

"I'd like to help. I want to stay around for the winter and spend time with Virnie."

"Great." But Conor wasn't sure what he thought. An extra man to help with the barn was good. But so long as Miles hung around he guessed he would get little chance to talk to Virnie. On the other hand, maybe it was what Virnie needed to realize she was worthy of love.

Christmas dinner was a true celebration. Diana had baked pies at home and brought them. The turkey, raised by Mrs. Jones, was tender and tasty. Conor wasn't sure where all the different vegetables and pickles had come from but guessed a great deal of it had been provided by Diana.

The meal over, they drew their chairs to the living area around the warm stove.

"This has been the best Christmas ever," Rae said.

Diana clapped her hands. "That gives me an idea. Why don't we each tell about the best Christmas we can remember?" She glanced eagerly around the group and when no one dissented she took it for agreement. "I'll start."

She sat back. "My best Christmas—apart from today—was the year my grandparents were all with us. It was the first time I remember all four of them being present. I just thought it was so special to have all that attention even if much of it went to my little brother who was just learning to walk. It was the year I got my favorite doll. She had a porcelain face and real hair and little black shoes. I still have her. In fact…" She darted a quick look at Gabe before she continued. "I brought her with me. Someday I hope to have a daughter to give it to."

Gabe laughed heartily, sending a flood of color to Diana's cheeks and Conor grinned at Rae. "Yup, a daughter is a pretty special gift."

Rae climbed to his lap and hugged him.

Virnie ducked her head and fiddled with her fingers.

Conor wanted to still her hands and assure her she was special even if her father hadn't believed it.

"Your turn, Gabe," Diana said.

He continued to smile at his wife. "It's easy for me to choose. The first Christmas I spent with you and your family after you agreed to be my wife."

"That was my worst," Diana whispered.

"Why?"

"Because you were leaving in a short time. Going West and I didn't know when I would see you again."

Gabe took her hands. "I had to find us our own place."

"I know. Go on and tell us why it was so special."

"Because of you. That's all."

Conor envied them their love. He forced himself to keep his gaze on them although he wanted nothing more than to look at Virnie and let her see the longing that made his eyes feel stark.

Gabe turned to Miles. "Care to share?"

Miles nodded. "The best Christmas I remember was when both our parents were alive and Virnie was about three. She was just learning to talk really well. Mother had made me socks and a new shirt.

She'd made Virnie a rag doll. I remember like it was yesterday how she cuddled that doll. I'm sure she was convinced it was real. She put it down to sleep wrapped in a blanket and turned to inform us all, 'Baby Sue is sleeping. You must be quiet.' Papa said he didn't think she'd mind us talking." He chuckled. "Virnie planted her hands on her hips and stood between us and her baby. 'She's my baby and I know what's best for her.' My how we did laugh."

The others chuckled to think of a tiny version of Virnie defending her doll.

Virnie stared at Miles. "I remember that doll." Her voice was barely a whisper. Her eyes widened and she gasped. "I remember Mama giving it to me." Her voice broke.

No one moved, sensing how special this moment was for Virnie. Conor's eyes stung. She'd wanted so badly to remember her mother, needed it to feel whole and loved. This could be the answer to his prayer on her behalf. He closed his eyes. His prayer was as much for him as for her. He understood she couldn't let herself love him until she found what her heart lacked.

"Do you have a favorite Christmas memory?" Diana asked her softly after a moment of silence. "If you don't want to say anything, we understand."

"No. I do. I remember that Christmas. I remember Papa and Mama laughing. I remember Mama hugging me when she gave me my baby." She turned to Miles. "It was real, you know. You'll never convince me otherwise."

Conor chuckled as did the others. Virnie had been a spunky child even as she was a strong woman. He knew with an assurance as strong as steel that she would find what she needed to heal her past.

Virnie turned to Conor. "And your best Christmas memory?"

He'd known this moment was coming. Yet every Christmas except this seemed tainted with disappointment or pain. So often growing up, survival had mattered more than gifts or celebration. Then after he married, his hopes for a loving home had been dashed by Irene's unhappiness. Only one thing had brightened those years—Rae. Suddenly he found a memory he cherished. He shifted Rae to one side of his lap so he could look into her eyes as he talked.

"Rae was about a year old. Just learning to walk really good. My parents had sent us gifts. And we'd bought her something. I think a ball but I'm not sure. In fact, I don't remember much about the gifts because all Rae cared about was the wrappings. She rattled them. She folded and unfolded them. She laughed as they made a crinkling noise. She wouldn't let us take them away even to go to bed." He smiled deeply at Rae. "You played with those pieces of paper until they were soft as cotton. You still had fragments of them when spring came."

"What happened to them, Pa?"

"You left them outside one night and it rained. In the morning they were nothing but mush."

"Aww."

He hugged her close. "You cried for an hour until finally your ma scooped up the remains and put them on a plate. They dried into an odd-shaped ball and you carried that until it completely disintegrated. In fact, I'm not totally sure there are specks of it still in the bottom of your drawer."

"Oh, Pa."

"What a nice story," Diana said.

Conor caught Virnie watching him and smiled.

She smiled back though he detected a tremor in her lips.

I love you. He hoped she would read the silent message of his heart.

She lowered her eyes then stole a quick glance. Her gaze was cautious but not resistant.

It was a good sign.

Chapter Fourteen

The men began work on the barn the next day. Miles insisted Virnie accompany him to the farm. Not that it took much convincing. She didn't want to miss a moment with Miles.

And this allowed her a perfectly acceptable way to spend time with Conor. And Rachael. Gabe and Diana, too, of course, she added hastily.

Having Miles visit, remembering Mama, feeling that she might have been loved by her parents had started to scrape back the shell she had built around her heart. She wasn't sure yet what lay beneath, whether it was something she would welcome or something dark and fearful. And that kept her from responding to the love she saw in Conor's eyes each time he looked at her. Not until she faced the depths of her heart could she accept love.

Little by little, with Miles's help, she was

rediscovering pieces of her childhood. He'd described the house they lived in. He told her of aunts and uncles she'd forgotten. He reminded her of Papa's job working in the livery barn.

"He loved horses," Miles said as he and Conor took a break from work. Gabe and Diana had gone to town, taking Rachael with them, to get some needed supplies. "He especially loved the big work horses. Virnie, do you remember him taking us to the barn to show us the horses?"

She shook her head. There was only one thing she clearly remembered about her father. "Why did Papa send me away?"

"Miss Price convinced him he wasn't being fair to you. Said he was allowing you to grow up a little hooligan." He said the word like it was poisonous on his tongue. "Papa found the word so offensive he could hardly talk. Even so, at first he resisted. But Miss Price was persuasive so he eventually agreed. He didn't want to."

Virnie found it hard to believe he had cared. "He said I should have been a boy."

Miles stared at her. "I can't imagine it but if he did I suppose it was because it would have been easier to leave you with me if you were."

Virnie ducked her head, pretending to have something on her fingernail. Her heart pounded with unshed tears and a bolt of fear that she could not deny. Her father had sent her away. Ripped her from her family all because he regretted she wasn't a boy. How could she trust someone to give her the love and acceptance she ached for when her own father couldn't? But was it because he didn't love her? The question roared through her head. It echoed in the silent absence of an answer. Without looking at Miles or Conor, she slipped from the table and pulled out pots and pans to make supper. Though she had no idea why she needed every pot in the cupboard.

The barn was almost finished. Tomorrow Gabe and Diana would return home. Miles announced he had found a job helping a farmer to the west who had broken his leg.

Virnie knew her time of being able to come to the farm would end when Miles left. She could hardly bear the thought. Although she couldn't trust herself to Conor's love, neither could she imagine not seeing him every day, not being aware of his watchfulness nor catching glimpses of his love.

If only she could figure out a way to fix what was wrong with her heart.

At first, when Miles triggered so many memories, she thought she had. But the time of feeling better had been short and transitory. Yes, she appreciated being able to remember her mother. She would always cherish that. But it wasn't enough.

And she didn't know what was.

The next day they went to the farm early to bid Gabe and Diana goodbye.

They stood admiring the raw new barn. "Thanks for all your help," Conor said, including both Miles and Gabe. "Looks good standing there strong and solid."

Strong and solid, Virnie thought. Just as he expected people to be.

Gabe glanced at the sky. "I hope we get home before this nice spell breaks."

They all looked skyward knowing how quickly a deadly winter storm could blow in.

"It looks good for the day. That should see you home," Conor said. "Godspeed. We'll see you in the spring."

Diana hugged Virnie. "We'll see you, too?"

"I'll be here until the end of the school term for certain." She caught Conor's gaze and saw stark disappointment because she hadn't promised so much more.

She held his gaze a moment. She wanted him to know she regretted how she felt. Suddenly she turned away. Seems like all her life she'd been trying to apologize for failing to be something she wasn't. Only in the classroom did she feel differently. Only there was she accepted as a competent human being. It was a good thing school was to resume in three days.

Gabe and Diana climbed into their wagon and

drove away. Rachael ran after them until Gabe waved her back.

Miles, Conor and Virnie stared until they were out of sight.

It would be lonely around here without them.

Miles stretched. "Come on, Conor, I'll help you move the rest of the things into place. I told Mr. Andrews I would be at his place tomorrow in time to do the chores. His wife has been trying to manage but with a baby and all it's too much."

"Let's get it done." Conor spun away.

Her heart heavy with regret, Virnie returned to the house. She couldn't give Conor what he needed but she'd make up for her failure by making an especially nice supper. She ached clear through at the thought that once Miles left she wouldn't be free to visit here.

Conor came while she was cooking.

Virnie glanced up. "Where's Miles?"

"Showing Rae something about teaching her pony tricks. I wanted a chance to speak to you alone."

She sent him a warning look.

"Virnie, I promised I would give you all the time you needed. And I mean to keep that promise. But can you offer me any hope?" He rushed on without giving her a chance to speak. "I thought seeing Miles would make you feel better. It's obvious he loves you and he talks about how much your parents loved you. Isn't that enough?"

She shook her head.

He held out his hands in a pleading gesture. "What do you need?"

"I don't know." She pushed the words past the pain tightening her throat and squeezing her lungs. Suddenly the words flowed like water from a broken dam. "All my life I've felt like I didn't measure up. I could never be what anyone wanted. My papa didn't think I was good enough. I guess I wonder if I will ever be good enough."

Miles stepped into sight.

She hadn't heard him enter the house and grew silent. She knew her inability to believe their father had loved her hurt him.

He shed his coat and snow-covered boots before he stepped to her side. "Virnie, you have to understand how hard Papa tried but you pushed him away."

"I don't remember that." She skidded her gaze back to Conor. Would he condemn her for Mile's announcement? But all she saw was sympathy.

"It's like you blamed him." Miles drew her attention back to him.

"For what?"

"Mama being gone."

"Why would I do that?"

"You were only five. How could you understand why your mama had left you? And then you got left alone or sent with me. It really upset your world."

She couldn't swallow as she remembered the fear of being alone in the corner of the room. Mama gone. Papa gone. Miles gone. And then Papa came back. Sudden hot uncontrollable anger surged up her throat. Anger that Papa had left her alone. She spun around so neither Conor nor Miles could see the anger she knew would surely be drawing her face into harsh lines. Then she remembered another time of anger. She flung around to spill the words at Miles.

"He said he wished I was a boy. He sent me away. He never wrote or let you write."

Miles reached for her but she backed away.

He dropped his hand. "He wanted to. But Miss Price had insisted if he let her take you we must never contact you. He wrote one letter anyway but Miss Price returned it with 'Don't do this again' scrawled across the envelope."

Virnie didn't believe him. She glowered at Miles and sent Conor a look full of skepticism. "Why would she do that?"

"She said it was best if you forgot your past."

Virnie couldn't deny the truth of those words. She'd heard them many times from Miss Price. She could only rock her head back and forth, trying to sort out her feelings.

Conor pulled her to his side, one arm across her shoulders. The weight and warmth of his arm settled her churning emotions.

"Papa always said it was for the best but it about killed him to send you away."

"I don't believe you."

"On his dying bed Papa said if I ever see you I was to tell you these words. Say, 'I regret sending her away. She would have turned out fine without Miss Price. She already had the makings of a good strong, resourceful woman. I was proud of her and her mama would have been, too.'"

Virnie turned her face into Conor's chest and clung to his shirtfront. Tears did not come. They couldn't escape the cages of her heart. Why had Miss Price insisted she never see her father again? Why did she think it was for the best? Had he sent her away because she shut him out? Was it all her fault?

She straightened, brushed her hair off her face and stepped away from Conor's hold. "You're only saying that to make me feel better, aren't you?"

"Oh, Virnie, I'm not. He loved you. Mama loved you. I loved you."

"So it was all my fault because I shut out Papa?"

Miles lifted his hands in a resigned gesture.

Conor again reached for Virnie but she shrugged away from being held. He met her eyes and searched hard and deep. She closed her heart and thoughts to him.

Conor sighed. "Virnie, must someone be made

to blame? Can you not accept that your father did what he thought was best? Miss Price, too? I don't think anybody in your life meant to make you feel unaccepted, or unimportant. Maybe it's time to take the good that every one of them gave you and turn it into what you want it to be. I know it's time you saw yourself as you really are—a strong, capable woman who can be loved and admired solely because of who she is."

She searched his eyes for truth. Found love and acceptance. Found it in him but not in herself. She stepped back. "It's easy to say. Hard to do."

"Can you at least think about it? Consider it possible?"

She couldn't turn from the longing and trust and certainty in his gaze. "I'll try."

"Virnie?"

She turned to face her brother.

"Conor is right. No one meant to hurt you. Everyone thought they were doing what was best for you. Forgive Papa. Forgive me. I should have stood up to Papa. I didn't want you to go."

She went to him and hugged him. "One thing I have never doubted was that you liked me."

He squeezed her hard. "Silly goose. I love you. What's more, I am proud of you and always have been. You've been a fighter since day one. Remember that as you sort through all this."

She straightened, swiped at her eyes. Felt Conor's

hand on her shoulder. It seemed natural to go to his arms for a hug from him, too. She knew he silently reiterated Miles's words.

She allowed herself to believe in his love. For the space of two heartbeats.

Then she pulled away. She longed to accept what Conor offered, to believe how Miles explained the past, but her heart simply would not allow it.

She and Miles left directly after supper. Thankfully Miles didn't try to continue the conversation about Papa.

The next morning, he rode by the Maxwells' to say goodbye. "I hate to leave you especially when—" He shrugged.

"I'll be all right. I just need to sort things out in my head."

"Conor is a good man."

"I know that."

"Don't shut him out."

He didn't say it but she heard the words inside her head. *Like you did Papa.*

"Remember what he said."

"You've both given me much to think about."

"I'll be back on Sunday, weather permitting. We'll talk more then." He hugged her one last time before he rode away.

She trod back to her bedroom and closed the door for privacy. She needed to sort out her thoughts. She wanted to. Instead rejection, hope, disappointment, blame all twisted inside her like a prairie tornado. She could no more separate one from the other than she could turn a tornado around.

School started again Monday and she welcomed the rhythm of the days. She had only one regret. Now that Rachael had her own pony, Conor no longer gave her a ride to school. Perhaps it was for the best. It would give her a chance to sort out her feelings.

Only by Saturday she was no closer to understanding why she couldn't put the past behind her and allow herself a new future, one full of love and belonging.

She kept busy Saturday with chores, hoping she could chase away her confusion. Several times she realized she paused to look out the window in the direction of the Russell farm. If Miles came perhaps they could go there for a visit. She hadn't seen Conor in eight days. She missed him more than made sense considering she continued to hold him off.

Late Saturday afternoon the weather reminded them they were in the midst of a Dakota winter. A storm blew in that obliterated the view out the window. The wind howled endlessly. Snow beat against the side of the house and plastered the outside of the window.

Mr. and Mrs. Maxwell huddled close to the stove

in the little living room. "You're welcome to join us, dear," Mrs. Maxwell said.

Her room was frigid so Virnie gathered together her lesson materials and pulled close to the fire.

Sunday, the storm still raged. When she considered venturing out to church, Mr. Maxwell stopped her. "Ye'd be lost before you got there. Best stay home and enjoy a quiet day."

Reluctantly, she agreed. She didn't want a quiet day. At least not here. However, she knew Miles wouldn't venture out. Nor would Conor and Rachael. She tried not to picture them snuggled together close to their little stove. No doubt Rachael would play with Tippy and the doll Diana had given her. What did Conor do on such afternoons? She imagined sitting with them and talking softly of dreams and wishes.

She slammed shut the book she was reading.

Both Mr. and Mrs. Maxwell jumped.

"My dear, what's the matter?" Mrs. Maxwell asked.

"Sorry. It slipped." She returned to a story that made no sense. She had dreams and wishes. They included sharing home and family with Conor. So why couldn't she just accept what he offered?

But by the time she slipped away to go to bed she was no closer to sorting out her feelings.

The storm continued Monday. Mr. Nelson came by and said she didn't need to go to the school. He would go by just in case some foolhardy parent had sent their child.

Virnie wondered how she would keep herself busy through another stormbound day. She wrote Miss Price a letter, finding it hard to communicate with the woman who had been the cause of Virnie never being able to see her father again. She sighed. Miss Price only did what she thought best. How was she to know the hurt it inflicted on Virnie's heart? She must try to explain how it had affected her. Perhaps in doing so she could help Miss Price to change. Certainly continue to give girls a chance for a better life but not at the expense of making them feel abandoned by their family.

"Perhaps you'd like to unravel this old pair of socks," Mrs. Maxwell said after Virnie had sighed loudly several times. "Most of the yarn is still fine."

"Certainly." She was more than grateful to have something to do.

She almost cheered when she wakened Tuesday morning to a clear blue sky and sun so bright off the new snow that it hurt her eyes.

"Better bundle up," Mr. Maxwell advised as she prepared to leave for school. "It's cold enough to freeze you." He wrapped several scarves around his neck and face as he got ready to head for work in the little government office where he filled out land titles and other documents.

Virnie added a scarf and a pair of mittens to her wardrobe. She gasped when she stepped outside. The cold penetrated her layers long before she dashed into the schoolroom.

Mr. Nelson was there, the fire already warming the room. "I'll shovel a path to the barn and outhouses. Don't expect too many children today."

He was right. Only three showed up. None who had to walk or ride any distance.

By the end of the week, she ached for the sight of Conor. The weather had moderated slightly but she didn't know if Miles would be able to come to town. Or if she'd get a chance to see Conor.

When Miles came to the door Sunday morning in time to escort her to church, she hugged him fiercely.

"Missed me, did you?"

"You might say so."

She took his arm as they stepped out to head for church. As they neared the building, she glanced about hoping to see Conor and Rachael.

"I think I'm not the only one you missed."

"What do you mean?" She tried to sound disinterested but Conor and Rachael turned into the yard just then and she feared she'd let a bit of excitement edge her voice.

Miles chuckled. "I'm taking it that you've sorted out your feelings for him."

"My feelings for him were never a problem."

He stopped to stare at her. "I don't understand. If you love him and he loves you, what is the problem?"

She slid her gaze past his shoulder and tried to sort out an answer. Here she was a teacher, supposedly of reasonable intelligence, and she could find no words to explain her feelings.

Miles caught her shoulders and shook her gently. "Virnie, what's wrong?"

"The only problem is me. I'm afraid to trust anyone to keep loving me." Her voice dropped to a whisper. "I'm afraid I'll disappoint them."

"Oh, Virnie, how could you think such a thing? I love you just as you are. I'm sure Conor does, too. Just accept it."

She nodded. He couldn't begin to understand how much she wished it were possible. Just accept it. She was grateful they had arrived at the doorway to the church.

Conor waited, Rachael at his side. He smiled, his eyes sought and found hers and his smile went from his mouth to her heart. He leaned close. "I've missed you."

"Me, too," she whispered, then straightened and let Miles escort her down the aisle to a pew. She hadn't forgotten the disapproval she'd earned by being careless about how she acted.

Conor seemed to understand and let Rachael

in to sit next to Virnie then slipped in beside his daughter.

Virnie was very conscious of his presence. Something shifted in her as if her heart had developed a will of its own, demanding she listen to it but she knew she must sort out her warring emotions before she gave in to the urging of her heart.

Conor turned slightly, saw how she glanced at him and his expression filled with promise and love.

This was what she wanted.

What she'd wanted all her life.

But…

The preacher rose to announce the first hymn.

Virnie focused her attention on the front, her eyes lingering on the cross carved in the front of the pulpit. God must surely know what she needed. And what better place to seek and find it than right here?

"Let us pray," the preacher said.

Virnie didn't hear his prayer as she silently voiced her own. *God, show me what it is I need in order to be free to accept Conor's love.*

Chapter Fifteen

"**Y**ou'll come to the farm?" Conor asked Miles, but his eyes reached for Virnie.

"Certainly. Expected we would. Mr. Brown said I might borrow his buggy."

Virnie turned to accompany her brother down the aisle.

Conor waited to whisper in her ear as she passed, "You and I need to talk."

She slipped past. She'd hoped for some wonderful insight as she listened intently to the sermon. But the preacher seemed to be stuck on one verse: "We are fearfully and wonderfully made." The words mocked her. She felt like God had made a mistake in creating her. She could never measure up to what others expected of her.

How could she ever trust love with Conor as long as she felt this way? She should refuse to go to the farm but she could no more deny herself an afternoon with Conor than she could erase her troubled thoughts. Although she tried. How she tried.

Conor and Rachael reached the farm before Miles and Virnie and as Virnie stepped into the house, she saw the table set and a pot of soup on the stove.

"I made the soup," Rachael announced.

Virnie dismissed her troubled thoughts in the pleasure of sharing this day and in her joy in seeing how far Rachael had come. She hugged Rachael. "Good for you."

Rachael ducked her head and giggled. "Pa helped some."

Virnie met Conor's eyes over Rachael's head and something at once demanding and promising filled his gaze. She slowly straightened, never breaking eye contact, wondering what his look meant, knowing she didn't want to disappoint him but fearing she would.

After lunch, Rachael begged them to come see the tricks she'd taught Prince so they trouped out to the barn. She'd taught her pony to bow and tap his hoof three times when she asked him how much was one plus two.

Virnie clapped, as did Miles and Conor.

"What other things can I teach him?" Rachael asked Miles.

Miles circled Rachael and her pony. "Hmm. Let's see."

Rachael shot her father a shy look. "Pa, I want it to be a surprise."

"Are you trying to get rid of me?"

"No. Well, maybe just for a little while."

Conor laughed. "Well, fine. Virnie and I will go for a walk." He took her hand and pulled it through his arm. "You'll be warm enough?"

"I think so." If he held her close to his side like this the warmth from his arm would drive away cold both from the outside and the inside of her body.

They meandered around the yard, Conor pointing out improvements he intended to make. They paused at the garden spot. "Next year I am going to take care of the garden." He shook his head. "Can't imagine why I neglected it in the past. I never want Rae to wonder where the next meal will come from."

He'd told her how his family had struggled to survive when he was growing up.

"I figure if a person works hard and is diligent, he can carve out a solid home on the prairies."

She was glad he chose to talk about the farm and his plans. They left the garden area and walked toward the first field, as far as the snow allowed them. "Land. Lots of land." He swept his arm to indicate the endless prairie.

He lowered his arm, pressed his hand to hers, covering it against his forearm. Filling her with warmth and love. If she could capture the assurance she felt standing next to him, listening to his dreams and plans, and pour it into her heart and cork it there…

She sighed. They didn't make corks for hearts.

Conor shifted to face her fully. He trailed his finger across her jawline. He gazed into her eyes with such warmth and longing she lowered her eyes and studied his chin. He'd shaved recently, probably before church, leaving only a dark shadow on his face. His face had strong line. When he smiled, deep crevasses gouged his cheeks. He didn't smile now. She lifted her gaze to his eyes, saw the warmth and hunger in them. She swallowed hard.

"Virnie, you must know I love you."

She nodded. "I know," she whispered. With love came expectations. That's what filled her with trembling fear.

"How do you feel about me?" The agony in his voice filled her with sorrow.

She didn't want to hurt him. Now or ever. "Conor, I love you."

He took her shoulders and held her inches from his embrace. "Then marry me. Share my life and my dreams."

She pressed her lips together. She could think of nothing in this world she wanted more. "I can't."

"Why?" He shook her gently, his voice almost a moan.

"How do I know I can be what you want me to be? How do you?"

He tucked his chin in and blinked at her. "I only want you to be you. Nothing else."

She rocked her head back and forth. "It's never been enough. Papa wanted me to be a boy. Miss Price wants me to be a teacher and a lady. You…" She sucked back air. "You want me to be strong. You expect it of everyone you care about, even yourself."

He pulled her to his chest and groaned. "Virnie, I confess that's all I wanted a few months ago. You taught me that it isn't enough. And when I waited for rescue, I realized two together are stronger than one alone. We balance each other. I thought I'd made that clear then. I did tell you, didn't I?"

"Yes." Her voice was muffled against his coat.

"You don't believe me?"

She edged back, steeling herself to leave the comfort of his chest, forcing herself to face the disappointment in his face. "I believe you."

"But…?"

"You would learn to despise my weaknesses." She clutched his lapels, afraid he would turn away in disgust.

He smiled. Trailed his gaze over her face as if memorizing every detail. He smiled. "I think I would only find them endearing."

She shook her head, knowing at some point he would realize she wasn't what he expected.

"Virnie, my sweet, sweet girl, you only have to be what you are. Nothing more. Nothing less. Just be what God created you to be."

"That's too simplistic."

His eyes brimmed with disappointment.

She ducked her head. She couldn't bear to see it starting already. "I'm trying to change. Perhaps in time…"

"How long must I wait?"

"I can't say."

"How will I know when you're ready?"

"I'll tell you."

He sighed. "I hate waiting, loving you but not being able to share my life with you." He pulled her against his chest again and held her like he never wanted to let her go.

She hated hurting him but feared she would hurt him worse if she agreed to marry him. How could she live up to his expectations?

They returned to the house and played a game of dominoes with Rachael and Miles. She did her best to disguise her inner turmoil and sensed Conor did the same. Several times she felt his gaze on her but she refused to look at him.

As they prepared to leave, Conor pulled her aside. "I will be patient but please don't make me wait too long." The way his voice cracked filled her with agony. "Virnie, I will pray for you to find the truth you need to discover about yourself."

She hesitated. Did he know what that truth was? She dismissed the thought. Even if he did, having him say it wouldn't convince her. She must discover what she needed on her own.

Miles left as soon as they returned to town.

Virnie retreated to her bedroom. She tried to think. She prayed for God to show her what her problem was.

But three days later she was no closer to feeling like she had settled her problem.

Wednesday night she excused herself early from the living room and the company of Mr. and Mrs. Maxwell. Tonight she intended to wrestle her inner turmoil into submission with God's help.

She opened her Bible and spread it on her bed and fell on her knees. *Lord, show me what I need to know.*

What did everyone expect of her? Why couldn't she please them?

Surely God had something to say about that.

She searched the pages of the Bible where it lay before her. It had fallen open to Psalms. In fact, to the very chapter the pastor had preached on the past Sunday.

I will praise Thee; for I am fearfully and wonder-

fully made. It was the end of the column and she paused.

Doubts flooded her mind. But not wanting to face them, she shifted her gaze to the top of the next column and continued to read.

Marvelous are Thy works; and that my soul knoweth right well.

Only her soul did not know and believe that His creation of her was marvelous. She shifted back to the beginning of the verse.

I will praise Thee.

How could she praise God when she didn't believe her creation wasn't a mistake? She'd tried so hard to please people.

Try pleasing God, being what He created you to be.

Who had He created her to be? A girl who should have been a boy? A young woman trying to forget her tough upbringing? Yet without it she wouldn't have been able to rescue Conor.

She froze.

Something bright and inviting hovered at the edges of her thoughts. Had God used everything in her life to make her into a unique individual with strengths that served her well—a teacher, a lady and yet with a core of strength that came from following Miles around? Or perhaps had been hers since birth?

Had she been trying to please the wrong people?

Happiness begins and ends with God. She'd heard the words or read them somewhere, the source long forgotten. And at the time she thought only about how nice the statement sounded but now it drove deep into her brain.

I have loved you with an everlasting love.

A sob caught at the roof of her mouth. *God, I thank You and praise You for making me. For creating me with individual strengths and weaknesses. I never realized before how all these things have prepared me to be a wife, a helpmate for Conor and a pioneer in this new, challenging land.* She buried her face against the rough chenille coverlet and let waves of joy and acceptance wash over her.

She lost track of time, until her knees started to remind her of the hard floor and she realized how cold she'd grown. She plucked a quilt from the foot of the bed and wrapped it around her as she curled up on the bed. She read the passage in the Psalms over and over. Each time she had to dash away fresh tears. Tears of joy and gratitude.

She was ready to share Conor's love and life.

Conor sat in the easy chair beside the stove, trying to force his attention to the farming publication before him. He'd struggled long and hard to be patient about Virnie. He knew he must trust God but found it easier to say than to do.

He abandoned all pretense at reading and tossed the paper to the side table. Rae had gone to bed. He was completely alone. Even Tippy insisted on sleeping with Rae. Shows how lonely a man was when he wished for a cat to keep him company.

He was tired of being alone. There was a time he was sure he could manage on his own. But he no longer wanted to. He wanted to share his life with Virnie.

If only he could do something to convince her she was all he wanted and needed. Just as she was. But he understood she carried some unreasonable fears she needed to deal with. He'd help her if he could or if she'd let him. But until she asked him to… well, all he could do was pray.

Sunday came and when Conor showed no indication of getting ready to attend the service, Rae stood in front on him. "Aren't we going to church?"

"Not today. It's too cold."

"It's not—" Seeing the warning in his face, she didn't finish. She stomped to her room where he heard her discussing it with Tippy. "It's not a bit cold. He just doesn't want to go."

No. He didn't. He couldn't face Virnie and know he must wait for her to change. Or did he mean, wait for God to work in her life? Whichever it was he decided he preferred to hole up at his farm until it happened.

The next Sunday he again told Rae he thought it was too cold to attend church. She retreated to the barn to spend time with her pony. At least she had the company of her pets.

He made a sugar and cinnamon sandwich for himself at lunch time. Rae hadn't come in. He guessed she'd come when she got hungry enough.

He stood at the stove wondering if it was worth the effort to make tea when he heard the sound of an approaching buggy. He peeked out the frosty window.

Miles and Virnie. Was she intent on tormenting him?

He watched Miles help Virnie down. She said something to him and he nodded and led the horse to the barn.

Conor steeled himself to face her. He must find things to converse about when he wanted to discuss only one thing—their love.

She knocked.

When had it come to this? She used to walk in like it was her home.

He called, "Come in."

Slowly the door opened. She stepped in and faced him across the space of the living area. Her eyes flooded with a joy that she seemed barely able to restrain. "I'm ready."

He blinked. What was that supposed to mean?

She grinned. "I told you I'd let you know when I was ready. I'm telling you now."

He remembered. He'd asked how he would know when she was ready to accept love. She said she'd tell him. "You mean…?" Dare he hope?

She nodded, her eyes shining like they'd captured the brilliant winter sun and carried it indoors.

He took one step, uncertain if it was real. She nodded and he knew it was. He closed the distance between them in two long strides, caught her to his chest and hugged her to his heart—where love had unlocked all his secret longings.

After a couple of minutes, he led her to the easy chair and sat down. He pulled her to his lap. "Are you ready to be happy?"

She rubbed her cheek against him. "I am happy."

He caught her chin and turned her to face him. "Are you ready to let me be part of your happiness?"

She nodded. "More than ready."

He kissed her. He'd wanted to do this for a very long time. He let his lips linger a moment. He'd have the rest of his life to enjoy kissing her. He shifted her to his shoulder so he could talk. "When can we get married?"

She sat up to face him, her expression serious. "I want to finish out my school year."

"But why? You don't have to prove anything to anyone, especially Miss Price."

"I'm not trying to be live up to her plans but still I do owe her for what she did for me. Because of her I am who I am."

He nodded, knowing she had finally found peace with the events of her past.

"Besides. I need time to learn to be whole—following the life God has planned for me instead of trying to be who I thought would please Papa or Miss Price." She seemed distracted by trailing her finger along his chin—a touch that made it impossible for Conor to think.

She removed her finger, curled her hands together in her lap. "'I am fearfully and wonderfully made.' I realize God used everything in my life to uniquely prepare me to be a pioneer wife."

"I love you, Virnie. I'm tired of being alone but I can wait if that's what you want."

"First, I have to talk to Mr. Nelson and the rest of the board. I'll tell them exactly what my intentions are—to finish the school year and then marry you. If they find that unacceptable, well, I refuse to pretend I don't love you."

He hugged her close then claimed her lips. His love for her filled him until he had to break away from their kiss to shout, "I love you, Virnie White. Now and always."

He pulled her to her feet and danced her around

the room. Paused at the door. "What happened to Miles?"

"I asked him to wait in the barn."

He swung her off her feet then put her down and kissed her soundly. "How long until the school year ends?"

Chapter Sixteen

June finally arrived. The intervening months had been both a delight and agony. Agony as Virnie and Conor waited to unite their lives. Rachael knew of the upcoming plans but at the request of the school board, they had told no one except their families. The delight had been in getting to know each other better. Conor had opened up every corner of his heart to her.

More than once he'd laughed as he shared something new. "I never told anyone else this."

She hugged the delight to herself. And she grew more and more confident in accepting who she was, who God had created her to be and in trusting Conor's love for her.

Much of her wedding preparations had been done in secret in order to fulfill the requirements of the school board. Not until a few weeks ago had she informed Miss Price, dreading the disappointment she knew she must cause.

After a long delay, the reply came back.

It is with a heavy heart that I read your news and yet I am not surprised. Although you could be an excellent, dedicated teacher I think I always sensed you wanted something else. If this is what you want and what makes you happy, then by all means pursue your dream. I do hope you will see fit to send me an invite to your wedding.

Virnie had been only too happy to do so. Miss Price had arrived in town yesterday in plenty of time for Virnie to show her the schoolhouse and discuss the successes of her year as a teacher. Then she had taken her to the farm and introduced Conor and Rachael.

Conor was cool at first. Virnie understood that he feared seeing Miss Price would cause Virnie's old fears to surface. She shared some of his trepidation. But she felt only pride and love as she showed Miss Price around.

"You are far more suited to this life than I could have guessed," Miss Price said later.

Today was her wedding day and she knew nothing but joy and anticipation.

Rachael waited with her in the little cloakroom of the church, pirouetting to make the bright yellow of her skirts whirl around. "I'm like a buttercup," she said.

"You're beautiful. Your pa will be so proud."

Rachael stopped spinning and stared at Virnie. "You're beautiful. Pa won't see anyone but you."

Virnie giggled and hugged Rachael. "I'll be sure and tell him to take note of you."

Rachael giggled, too. "It doesn't matter. Getting you for a ma is the best thing of all."

Virnie kissed the child. "I love you."

"I love you, too, Mama. It is all right if I call you that now?"

"Perfect."

Miles knocked and entered the room. "Ready?"

"Ready and waiting." She took his arm and they followed Rachael down the aisle.

Conor stood at the front so handsome it made her heart hurt. He wore the gray tie she'd given him at Christmas. It made his blue eyes brighter, stronger. And the smile he gave her made her knees go suddenly weak. Miles covered her hand as it rested on his forearm and gave her a concerned glance.

She forced strength to her limbs and lifted her head.

This was the best day of her life.

Later, after they'd exchanged vows and kissed for

the first time as man and wife, she clung to him. "I love you," she whispered as they rushed down the aisle.

His eyes filled with tender amusement. "I know."

* * * * *

Dear Reader,

I love being able, as a writer, to rescue lonely men and women and their children and put them into loving families. It seems to be an oft-repeated theme in my books. And in my life, too. I've been blessed with a loving, large family. Growing up, I always envied those families who sat down for special meals with a whole crowd of brothers, sisters, aunts, uncles, cousins and grandparents, so one of the things I enjoy is hosting big family dinners. Yes, our house is small but we manage. And in the summer when we can spread out across our big yard is even more special.

I love the verse in Psalm 68:6. "God sets the lonely in families." I pray that as you read Virnie and Conor's story you will learn a new appreciation of your particular family. If you are unfortunate and don't have those kind of ties, I pray you will seek them out through church or other connections, and, like Virnie, allow others to love you.

I love to hear from my readers. You can contact me and check out my other books at www.lindaford.org.

Blessings,

Linda Ford

QUESTIONS FOR DISCUSSION

1. Virnie's mother died when she was young. How did her father cope? How did that affect her?

2. Virnie was negatively impacted by the events that saw her placed with the teacher. Why? How have they shaped her thoughts?

3. Conor's childhood had also shaped him. What does he want and why?

4. How did he feel his first wife, Irene, failed him? How had this impacted his faith in life?

5. What was there about Conor that triggered memories that Virnie had tried to erase? How did she deal with this?

6. What made Virnie get involved with Conor and Rachael?

7. Were you aware of Virnie's strengths before she was? What clues revealed her strength? How was she uniquely equipped to deal with the crisis she faced?

8.   What part did Miles play in Virnie's healing? Was he able to make her past less painful? If she hadn't been able to find Miles, do you think she would have been stuck in her past?

9.   Even after Miles explained their father's reasoning to Virnie and assured her their father loved her, Virnie still wasn't free to love. Why not?

10.   Virnie lived under strict rules of conduct. Did she compromise them?

11.   Virnie was a faithful Christian. What things did she do to show you that? Why do you think it wasn't enough to make her overcome her past? What did she need to do?

12.   Conor promised to wait patiently. Do you think he would or could keep that promise if Virnie hadn't changed when she did?

13.   What event caused Conor to grow in his faith walk? How did he show he had changed?

14.   Do you think Virnie will need to remind herself of the lessons she's learned as she faces the challenges of being a farmer's wife?

15. Conor learned that needs don't make him weak. How do you think he will show that to Virnie as they live together?

HISTORICAL

TITLES AVAILABLE NEXT MONTH
Available April 12, 2011

YUKON WEDDING
Alaskan Brides
Allie Pleiter

THE LAWMAN CLAIMS HIS BRIDE
Charity House
Renee Ryan

AT THE CAPTAIN'S COMMAND
Louise M. Gouge

THE SHERIFF'S SWEETHEART
Brides of Simpson Creek
Laurie Kingery

LIHCNM0311

REQUEST YOUR FREE BOOKS!

2 FREE INSPIRATIONAL NOVELS
PLUS 2
FREE
MYSTERY GIFTS

Love Inspired
HISTORICAL
INSPIRATIONAL HISTORICAL ROMANCE

YES! Please send me 2 FREE Love Inspired® Historical novels and my 2 FREE mystery gifts (gifts are worth about $10). After receiving them, if I don't wish to receive any more books, I can return the shipping statement marked "cancel". If I don't cancel, I will receive 4 brand-new novels every month and be billed just $4.24 per book in the U.S. or $4.74 per book in Canada. That's a saving of at least 23% off the cover price. It's quite a bargain! Shipping and handling is just 50¢ per book in the U.S. and 75¢ per book in Canada.* I understand that accepting the 2 free books and gifts places me under no obligation to buy anything. I can always return a shipment and cancel at any time. Even if I never buy another book, the two free books and gifts are mine to keep forever.

102/302 IDN FDCH

Name	(PLEASE PRINT)	
Address		Apt. #
City	State/Prov.	Zip/Postal Code

Signature (if under 18, a parent or guardian must sign)

Mail to the **Reader Service:**
IN U.S.A.: P.O. Box 1867, Buffalo, NY 14240-1867
IN CANADA: P.O. Box 609, Fort Erie, Ontario L2A 5X3

Not valid for current subscribers to Love Inspired Historical books.

Want to try two free books from another series?
Call 1-800-873-8635 or visit www.ReaderService.com.

* Terms and prices subject to change without notice. Prices do not include applicable taxes. Sales tax applicable in N.Y. Canadian residents will be charged applicable taxes. Offer not valid in Quebec. This offer is limited to one order per household. All orders subject to credit approval. Credit or debit balances in a customer's account(s) may be offset by any other outstanding balance owed by or to the customer. Please allow 4 to 6 weeks for delivery. Offer available while quantities last.

Your Privacy—The Reader Service is committed to protecting your privacy. Our Privacy Policy is available online at www.ReaderService.com or upon request from the Reader Service.

We make a portion of our mailing list available to reputable third parties that offer products we believe may interest you. If you prefer that we not exchange your name with third parties, or if you wish to clarify or modify your communication preferences, please visit us at www.ReaderService.com/consumerschoice or write to us at Reader Service Preference Service, P.O. Box 9062, Buffalo, NY 14269. Include your complete name and address.

LIH11

*When David Foster comes across an unconscious woman
on his friends' doorstep, she evokes his natural born
instinct to take care of her.*

*Read on for a sneak peek of A BABY BY EASTER
by Lois Richer, available April, only from Love Inspired.*

"You could marry Davy, Susannah. He would look after
you. He looks after me." Darla's bright voice dropped. "He
had a girlfriend. They were going to get married, but she
didn't want me. She wanted Davy to send me away."

David almost groaned. How had his sister found out?
He'd been so careful—

"I'm sure your brother is very nice, Darla. And I'm glad
he's taking care of you. But I don't want to marry him. I
don't want to marry anyone," Susannah said. "I only came
to Connie's to see if I could stay here for a while."

"But Davy needs someone to love him. Somebody else
but me." Darla's face crumpled, the way it always did before she lost her temper. David was about to step forward
when Susannah reached out and hugged his sister.

"Thank you for offering, Darla. You're very generous. I
think your brother is lucky to have you love him." Susannah
brushed the bangs from Darla's sad face. "If I end up staying with Connie, I promise I'll see you lots. We could go to
that playground you talked about."

Susannah's foster sister Connie breezed into the room.
"I'm so glad to see you, Suze. But you're ill." She leaned
back to study the circles of red now dotting Susannah's
cheeks. "You're very pale. I think you need to see a doctor."

"I'm pregnant." The words burst out of Susannah in a
rush. Then she lifted her head and looked David straight in
the eye, as if awaiting his condemnation.

SHLIEXP0411R

But it wasn't condemnation David felt. It was hurt. He'd prayed so long, so hard, for a family, a wife, a child. And he'd lost all chance of that—not once, but twice.

How could God deny him the longing of his heart, yet give this ill woman a child she was in no way prepared to care for?

Although David has given up on his dream of having a family, will he offer to help Susannah in her time of need? Find out in A BABY BY EASTER, available April, only from Love Inspired.

Love Inspired®

Top authors

Janet Tronstad and Debra Clopton

bring readers two heartwarming stories,
where estranged sisters find family and love in
this very special collection celebrating motherhood!

Available April 2011.

www.SteepleHill.com